Teddy Fay returns to his roots in espionage in the latest thriller from #1 *New York Times*–bestselling author Stuart Woods.

When Teddy Fay receives a freelance assignment from a gentleman he can't refuse, he jets off to Paris on the hunt for a treasonous criminal. But as Teddy unearths more information that just doesn't seem to connect, his straightforward mission becomes far bigger—and stranger—than he could imagine. The trail of bread crumbs leads to secrets hidden within secrets, evildoers trading in money and power, and a global threat on an unprecedented scale. Under the beautiful veneer of the City of Lights, true villainy lurks in the shadows . . . and Teddy Fay alone can prevent the impending disaster.

Praise for the Stone Barrington Novels

Wild Card

"Woods shows no sign of flagging in this long-running series."   —*Publishers Weekly*

A Delicate Touch

"Woods continues to deliver satisfying escapist fare, with the Bondian Barrington outmaneuvering his foes yet again, always with high-tech gadgetry at the ready and a beautiful woman at his side."   —*Booklist*

Desperate Measures

"Woods creates another action-packed thriller for his readers to devour, with plenty of interesting twists and turns that make for a nonstop, can't-catch-your-breath read." —*Booklist*

Turbulence

"Inventive . . . [An] alluring world of wealth, power, and crime." —*Publishers Weekly*

Shoot First

"Smooth . . . The principal pleasure lies in watching the suave, resourceful Stone maintain his good humor and high lifestyle throughout all his travails."

—*Publishers Weekly*

Unbound

"Stuart Woods is a no-nonsense, slam-bang storyteller." —*Chicago Tribune*

Quick & Dirty

"Suspenseful . . . The excitement builds."

—*Publishers Weekly*

Indecent Exposure

"[An] irresistible, luxury-soaked soap opera."

—*Publishers Weekly*

Fast & Loose

"Another entertaining episode in [a] soap opera about the rich and famous." —Associated Press

Below the Belt

"Compulsively readable . . . [An] easy-reading page-turner."
—*Booklist*

Sex, Lies & Serious Money

"Series fans will continue to enjoy this bird's-eye view of the high life."
—*Booklist*

Dishonorable Intentions

"Diverting."
—*Publishers Weekly*

Family Jewels

"Mr. Woods knows how to portray the beautiful people, their manners and mores, their fluid and sparkling conversation, their easy expectations and all the glitter that surrounds and defines them. A master of dialogue, action and atmosphere, [Woods] has added one more jewel of a thriller-mystery to his ever-growing collection."
—*Florida Weekly*

Scandalous Behavior

"Addictive . . . Pick up [*Scandalous Behavior*] at your peril. You can get hooked."
—*Lincoln Journal Star*

Foreign Affairs

"Purrs like a well-tuned dream machine. . . . Mr. Woods knows how to set up scenes and link them to keep the action, emotion, and information moving. He presents the places he takes us to vividly and convincingly. . . . Enjoy this slick thriller by a thoroughly satisfying professional."
—*Florida Weekly*

Hot Pursuit

"Fans will enjoy the vicarious luxury ride as usual."

—*Publishers Weekly*

Insatiable Appetites

"Multiple exciting storylines . . . Readers of the series will enjoy the return of the dangerous Dolce."

—*Booklist*

Paris Match

"Plenty of fast-paced action and deluxe experiences that keep the pages turning. Woods is masterful with his use of dialogue and creates natural and vivid scenes for his readers to enjoy."

—Myrtle Beach *Sun News*

Cut and Thrust

"This installment goes down as smoothly as a glass of Knob Creek."

—*Publishers Weekly*

Carnal Curiosity

"Stone Barrington shows he's one of the smoothest operators around. . . . Entertaining."

—*Publishers Weekly*

Standup Guy

"Stuart Woods still owns an imagination that simply won't quit. . . . This is yet another edge-of-your-seat adventure."

—*Suspense Magazine*

Doing Hard Time

"Longtime Woods fans who have seen Teddy [Fay] evolve from a villain to something of a lovable antihero will enjoy watching the former enemies work together in this exciting yarn. Is this the beginning of a beautiful partnership? Let's hope so."   —*Booklist*

Unintended Consequences

"Since 1981, readers have not been able to get their fill of Stuart Woods's *New York Times* bestselling novels of suspense."   —*Orlando Sentinel*

Collateral Damage

"High-octane . . . Woods's blend of exciting action, sophisticated gadgetry, and last-minute heroics doesn't disappoint."   —*Publishers Weekly*

Severe Clear

"Stuart Woods has proven time and time again that he's a master of suspense who keeps his readers frantically turning the pages."   —Bookreporter.com

BOOKS BY STUART WOODS

FICTION

Stealth[†]

Contraband[†]

Wild Card[†]

A Delicate Touch[†]

Desperate Measures[†]

Turbulence[†]

Shoot First[†]

Unbound[†]

Quick & Dirty[†]

Indecent Exposure[†]

Fast & Loose[†]

Below the Belt[†]

Sex, Lies & Serious Money[†]

Dishonorable Intentions[†]

Family Jewels[†]

Scandalous Behavior[†]

Foreign Affairs[†]

Naked Greed[†]

Hot Pursuit[†]

Insatiable Appetites[†]

Paris Match[†]

Cut and Thrust[†]

Carnal Curiosity[†]

Standup Guy[†]

Doing Hard Time[†]

Unintended Consequences[†]

Collateral Damage[†]

Severe Clear[†]

Unnatural Acts[†]

DC Dead[†]

Son of Stone[†]

Bel-Air Dead[†]

Strategic Moves[†]

Santa Fe Edge[§]

Lucid Intervals[†]

Kisser[†]

Hothouse Orchid[*]

Loitering with Intent[†]

Mounting Fears[‡]

Hot Mahogany[†]

Santa Fe Dead[§]

Beverly Hills Dead

Shoot Him If He Runs[†]

Fresh Disasters[†]

Short Straw[§]

Dark Harbor[†]

Iron Orchid[*]

Two-Dollar Bill[†]

The Prince of Beverly Hills

Reckless Abandon[†]

Capital Crimes[‡]

Dirty Work[†]

Blood Orchid[*]

The Short Forever[†]

Orchid Blues[*]

Cold Paradise[†]

L.A. Dead[†]

The Run[‡]

Worst Fears Realized[†]

Orchid Beach[*]

Swimming to Catalina[†]

Dead in the Water[†]

Dirt[†]

Choke

Imperfect Strangers

Heat

Dead Eyes

L.A. Times

Santa Fe Rules[§]

New York Dead[†]

Palindrome

Grass Roots[‡]

White Cargo

Deep Lie[‡]

Under the Lake

Run Before the Wind[‡]

Chiefs[‡]

COAUTHORED BOOKS

Skin Game[**] *(with Parnell Hall)*

The Money Shot[**] *(with Parnell Hall)*

Barely Legal[††] *(with Parnell Hall)*

Smooth Operator[**] *(with Parnell Hall)*

TRAVEL

A Romantic's Guide to the Country Inns
of Britain and Ireland (*1979*)

MEMOIR

Blue Water, Green Skipper

[*]A Holly Barker Novel
[†]A Stone Barrington Novel
[‡]A Will Lee Novel
[§]An Ed Eagle Novel
[**]A Teddy Fay Novel
[††]A Herbie Fisher Novel

SKIN GAME

STUART WOODS
and Parnell Hall

G. P. Putnam's Sons

NEW YORK

PUTNAM
— EST. 1838 —

G. P. PUTNAM'S SONS
Publishers Since 1838
An imprint of Penguin Random House LLC
penguinrandomhouse.com

The Library of Congress has catalogued the G. P. Putnam's Sons
hardcover edition as follows:

Names: Woods, Stuart, author. | Hall, Parnell, author.
Title: Skin game / Stuart Woods and Parnell Hall.
Description: New York: G. P. Putnam's Sons, 2019.
Identifiers: LCCN 2018049556 | ISBN 9780735219168 (hardcover) |
ISBN 9780735219182 (ebook)
Subjects: | GSAFD: Suspense fiction.
Classification: LCC PS3573.O642 S59 2019 | DDC 813/.54—dc23
LC record available at https://lccn.loc.gov/2018049556
p.   cm.

First G. P. Putnam's Sons hardcover edition / June 2019
First G. P. Putnam's Sons premium edition / November 2019
G. P. Putnam's Sons premium edition ISBN: 9780735219175

Printed in the United States of America
1 3 5 7 9 10 8 6 4 2

SKIN GAME

1.

TEDDY FAY FINISHED his twenty laps in the terrace pool. He pulled himself out and sat on the deck, drinking in the morning sun.

His broken leg had nearly healed. Remarkable, considering the amount of stress he'd subjected it to before allowing it to be put in a cast. Or rather, put *back* in a cast. Extenuating circumstances had forced him to cut off the original cast in order to deal with a life-or-death situation. He'd been a good boy since, even followed his rehab regimen.

The fact that he liked swimming didn't hurt.

He got up, sat in a deck chair, and poured himself a cool glass of lemonade.

Teddy enjoyed the three-story split-level Hollywood house on Mulholland Drive that he'd purchased in the name of Billy Barnett. Teddy had three identities. That is . . . three *current* identities. In the course of his career, he had played many roles, occasionally more than one at a time, but they were usually temporary. As Billy Barnett, he had risen through the ranks from production assistant to producer at Centurion Studios. As Mark

Weldon, he was a stuntman who had evolved into a character actor who specialized in playing villains.

As Teddy Fay, he was not known at all.

His cell phone rang. Teddy scooped it up. "Hello?"

"Billy Barnett?"

"Yes."

"This is Lance Cabot."

Teddy nearly dropped the phone. Lance Cabot was the head of the CIA. Teddy had worked for Lance once, before going rogue and killing people who deserved to die. Lance had organized a global manhunt for him, but Teddy was so elusive they soon elevated him to the top of the Most Wanted list. When even a presidential pardon failed to cool the Agency's ardor, Teddy changed his name and dropped out of sight. He'd been rumored dead. Most agents subscribed to the rumor.

Teddy said, "Why would the head of the CIA be calling a Hollywood film producer?"

"I'm not calling you in your producer capacity."

Teddy paused. "Go on."

"We have a problem in Paris."

"Oh?"

"We have a mole. Which is ridiculous—there's nothing happening in Paris that would warrant an enemy power planting a mole at that branch. The Agency was tracking only one individual recently, a low-level Syrian agent named Hassan Hamui. Recently he suddenly dropped out of sight, as if he knew he was under surveillance: knew when, how, and by whom. That's why we think we have a mole."

"And you want someone to handle the situation? Well, I'm not the man you're looking for. I happen to know you went out of your way to try to kill him, so I'd hardly care to be that guy. But if you want me to apply my meager talents to the situation, perhaps we can work something out."

"You want money?"

"Hardly. I can't be bought because I have all I need. I'm not above doing a favor for a friend, but you hardly fit into that category."

"You're still alive, aren't you?"

"What do you mean by that?"

"If I wanted to, finding and killing you wouldn't be hard. After all, I made this phone call."

"Is that a threat?"

"Not at all. I'm pointing it out as a token of friendship, since such things seem to matter."

"What would I have to do?"

"Go undercover, assume a new identity. I know you've played everybody from a bag lady to a bank president, but this might be sort of a stretch."

"Oh? Who do I have to pretend to be?"

"A CIA operative."

"Thanks a heap."

"I need you to leave at once."

"Are you picking me up here?"

"No."

"Will you fly me from New York?"

"It shouldn't look like we brought you in. Our mole would go on high alert. It has to appear as if you're emerging from deep cover. Whoever you wish to be will suddenly appear in our records as if he'd been there all the time. You get to pick your own legend. Once you do, you might let me know who you are."

"You're saying no one's running me. There's no one in charge of this mission I can contact."

"Would you listen to them if there were?"

"What's my cover story?"

"It doesn't matter, just so you have one. We have a leak. We don't know how high or low it goes, but we can't be telling people who might *be* the leak that we're looking for the leak."

"I have to create my own cover, fly myself in, and make up my own assignment?"

"I thought you'd like that."

"Fuck you, too, Lance."

2.

A BAD RIPPED OFF his headset. This was the call he'd been waiting for. He was sure of it. Fahd Kassin would be pleased.

It was one thing to bug the phone of the most powerful man in the CIA. It was another to sit through the endless daily minutiae that flowed through his office. Abad was excited as he jammed a memory stick into the computer and began the transfer.

FAHD KASSIN WAS a bundle of nerves. The coup the Syrian strongman had been planning for months was on the horizon, and things were going wrong. How could it be? His agent had infiltrated the CIA station in Paris, and from all reports the Agency had no idea of his intentions. And yet, a spy was suspected. A *mole*, that was what they called it. They had no idea who it might be, but the fact they suspected anyone was cause for alarm.

Defensive measures were mandatory. Just for a couple more weeks. Just until he made himself the most powerful man in the world.

In the meantime, it was crucial that Syrian intelligence didn't become aware of his plan. Fahd Kassin's project was not officially sanctioned. It was not sanctioned at all.

There was a knock on the door.

"Come in."

A computer hacker entered. Fahd couldn't recall his name. He was one of the men assigned to monitor the phone and wiretaps.

"Yes?" Fahd said impatiently.

Even his tone could not dampen the hacker's excitement. "I got it! The call you wanted to be alerted to. The head of the CIA called a man in California. He told him there was a mole in the Paris office and asked him to take care of it."

"Who did he call?"

"A Mr. Billy Barnett."

"And who is 'Billy Barnett'?"

"A Hollywood producer."

Fahd frowned. "A *movie* producer?"

"That's right. The producer tried to claim he wasn't the man he was looking for."

"You recorded the conversation?"

"Yes. It's on this memory stick."

"I can listen to it here?"

"Yes."

"Show me."

The hacker plugged the memory stick into Fahd's computer. He opened the file of Lance's calls, and played back the last one.

Fahd said, "What are you doing about the movie producer?"

"When the director called him, I tuned in to his cell phone frequency."

"You can do that?"

"Yes. Do you want me to explain how?"

"No. You're telling me I can listen in to his calls from my computer?"

"Yes."

"Show me how."

The hacker plugged in Billy Barnett's phone number, and opened the channel. "He's not on the phone at the moment, but if he makes a call, you can hear it by clicking this tab."

"Good job. This could be important."

"Yes. I will write it up in detail."

"No need. You have reported it to me. I will take it from here."

"Of course, sir. It is your project. I will merely report the facts."

"You don't need to do that."

"It's no trouble."

Fahd frowned. It *was* trouble from his point of view. He had his own agenda, and there were certain things he did not wish known, even by his own minions.

This was one of them.

Fahd nodded. "Who else did you show this to?"

"No one. I put it on the memory stick and came right in."

"Good job. Show me again how I access his phone."

The hacker hunched over the computer.

Fahd pushed a button on his desk.

A short, squat man in a drab brown suit glided in the door on little cat feet. He stepped up behind the hacker, deftly removed a handgun from a shoulder holster under his coat, and shot him in the head.

The hacker collapsed on the keyboard.

Fahd flinched. He was afraid the man might hit the wrong key and close the program. But the hacker slid off the keyboard and slumped to the ground.

"I trust you'll deal with the body," Fahd said to Aziz.

Aziz didn't answer. He never spoke. Impassive as ever, he picked up the body of the hacker, threw him over his shoulder, and carried him out.

Fahd Kassin sat at the computer and looked at the screen the hacker had opened for him.

Fahd shook his head. "Billy Barnett."

3.

TEDDY FAY DROVE onto the back lot of Centurion Studios. The guard at the gate waved him in. Teddy was a well-known figure on the movie set. As producer Billy Barnett, he was a man of some importance. He even had his own parking space, though he still felt funny using it.

Teddy let himself in through the soundstage. Nothing was filming that day, and it was faster than walking around to the main entrance. Teddy made his way down the corridor to the production offices.

Peter Barrington was in his. The young director was in the earliest stages of preproduction for his next feature. The film hadn't even been cast yet.

Rita, his assistant, buzzed him over the intercom. "Billy Barnett's here."

"Send him in."

Billy found Peter at his desk huddled over a few pages of script.

"Working on a rewrite?" Teddy said.

Peter looked up and grinned. "Hi, Billy. The changes aren't for me. We're auditioning Liz Hampton for a role. She's a little long in the tooth for it, as written."

"You'd rewrite the part for her?"

"I would if we got her. It wouldn't hurt the story any, and she's one of those actresses who's box-office gold for good reason. People like to see her name in the credits because they know it means a good performance."

"Yeah. I notice there's no part for character actor Mark Weldon in the movie."

"There really isn't," Peter said. "I was hoping you'd be content with producing this one."

"I had another idea. I don't think you're getting all the credit you deserve. I would think 'produced, written, and directed by' would go a long way toward establishing you as an auteur."

Peter grinned. "Yeah, right. And maybe I'll do hair and makeup, too. Trust me, writing and directing is enough. So can I count on you?"

Teddy grimaced. "The thing is, I kind of have to do a favor."

"For a friend?"

"Not exactly. But it needs to be done. Can I have some time off?"

"You know you can."

"I don't want to presume."

"Billy. After everything you've done for me and this studio, you can do anything you want."

"Well, I might like to try my hand at music director."

"Except that."

"How about caterer?"

Peter grinned. "Go on. Get out of here."

4.

STONE BARRINGTON WAS having a drink in his office with Dino Bacchetti. As one might expect in a conversation between one of New York City's top attorneys and the New York City police commissioner, weighty matters were being discussed. At the moment, the bone of contention was where to have dinner.

In the past, it was always Elaine's. Since it closed, the choice was often Patroon, but tonight Dino was lobbying for Peter Luger, the famed Brooklyn steakhouse.

"I don't think so," Stone said.

"What do you have against Peter Luger?" Dino wanted to know.

"I have nothing against Peter Luger. It's too late to get a reservation."

"I'm the New York City police commissioner. Do you really think I can't get a reservation?"

"Wouldn't that be abuse of power?"

"Absolutely. It's the only reason I took the job."

"Aw, come on, Dino. Think of the people who will be canceled to make room."

"No one will be canceled. Someone will get crowded closer to the kitchen."

The phone rang. Stone scooped it up. "Hello?"

"Hi, Stone."

"Billy!" Stone said. Then to Dino, "Hey, Dino, it's Billy Barnett."

"Invite him to dinner," Dino said.

"Dino and I were just planning dinner."

"I'm in L.A."

"That makes it harder."

"Where are you going to go?"

"We were just talking about it. Dino's pushing Peter Luger."

"Wish I were there. I love their steak. Why are you arguing?"

"We don't have a reservation."

"And Dino thinks they'll serve him anyway?"

"Ever since they made him commissioner he's got a swelled head."

"Hey, I'm right here," Dino protested.

"So why did you call?" Stone said.

"Actually, I was calling about dinner," Teddy said. "I can't make it tonight, but how about tomorrow?"

"That would be great. Where do you want to eat?"

"Paris."

5.

FAHD KASSIN, WHO had been monitoring Billy
Barnett's calls, honed in on the word *Paris*. It put
him on high alert, and he listened to the rest of the conversation with eager anticipation.

He was disappointed. Billy Barnett failed to elaborate
on the comment, saying merely that he would see Stone
tomorrow.

Fahd threw down the headphones in disgust. Why
couldn't the man have been more explicit? Instead,
he'd hardly been any help at all. He'd referred to the man
he called as "Stone," probably a nickname, and they referred to a third man as the commissioner, though no
one said commissioner of what. He also had an unlikely
name, though Fahd couldn't recall it, he'd have to listen
to the recording again. Fahd didn't want to do that, he
wanted a lackey to do it for him. Only he'd had that
lackey shot.

All right. Billy Barnett was in Los Angeles, but the
number he'd called was in a different area code: 212. He
could look that up. More grunt work.

Fahd summoned one of the techies from the other room. The man came in rather hesitantly. The last techie summoned from that room had never returned.

"What's your name?"

"Joram."

Fahd handed him a piece of paper. "Trace this phone number, Joram. I want to know who owns it, and where he lives."

"Yes, sir."

As the techie scurried out, Fahd heard a ringtone sound coming from the headphones, indicating one of the lines he was tracking was making a call. He looked at the computer screen. It was Billy Barnett again. Fahd grabbed the headphones and jammed them on.

Fahd hoped he was calling his party back, but this time it was an eight hundred number. It rang twice before it was picked up.

"Thank you for calling American Airlines. If you are checking on a reservation, press one. If you are changing a reservation, press two. If you are making a new reservation, press three."

The recorded menu would have daunted most callers, but over the mechanical voice there came the touch tone sounds of Billy Barnett punching in some code or other, and almost immediately the line was answered by an actual human being.

"American Airlines reservations, this is Jeremy, how may I help you?"

Aside from taking Billy first, Jeremy treated him just like any other customer, and took his reservation.

When Billy hung up, Fahd smiled in satisfaction. At last he had something he could deal with.

Fahd took off the headphones and picked up the phone.

6.

DARBY WAS GLAD to get the call. His current assignment was dull work on behalf of a Syrian asset. No chance to hone his skills. Not that they needed honing. He was, and always had been, a first-rate assassin. A good soldier, he'd accepted the transfer; still, L.A. was a little like being put out to pasture. He'd been happier in Washington, D.C., where jobs were frequent. He heartily disagreed with the assessment that the capital had become too hot for him, though he kept that opinion to himself, of course. He moved to L.A., and waited for the job that never came.

He could hardly believe it had.

"Yes?"

"Billy Barnett just booked a seat on the red-eye to New York. See that he doesn't go."

"Is he listed?"

"Address on Mulholland Drive. You can google him for a picture."

"I know my job."

"Then why did you ask?"

Darby knew better than to answer. He took his medicine and waited.

"Call me when it's done."

The phone clicked dead.

Darby put on a shoulder holster and slipped in his gun. It was a brand-new throw-down piece, as were all his weapons. Ballistics would never link one hit of his to another.

Darby went to his computer and found a photo of Billy Barnett. He didn't bother to print it out. One glance and it was engrained in his memory.

He looked up Billy Barnett's address and checked the time of the flight's departure. It would be easier to kill him at home, but he wasn't necessarily there, and finding out that he wasn't would take too much time for comfort.

It didn't matter where Billy Barnett was now. He knew where he was going to be.

He'd have to take him out at the airport.

7.

TEDDY BREEZED RIGHT through the airport. The check-in line was long, but he was flying business class, so he zipped through the priority line. He checked his suitcase, collected his boarding pass, and headed for security. Billy Barnett had TSA precheck, so once again he skipped the line. He handed his boarding pass and photo ID to the TSA agent, was approved, and walked on toward the metal detector. He didn't even have to take off his shoes.

Darby watched in helpless frustration. His first assignment in months, and the man just walked away. He could not fail. He had to get through security.

Darby went back to check-in and got in the priority line. There was only one passenger ahead of him. He waited impatiently for the man to be done, then stepped up to the counter.

"One business class ticket to JFK."

"That flight is sold out."

"Check again."

The woman did. "Actually we have a late cancellation. I can put you on standby."

"Standby?"

"There is a waiting list."

"Put me on the top of it."

"I can't do that."

Darby palmed three hundred dollars across the counter. "Yes, you can."

The woman whisked the bills under the counter. "May I have your credit card and photo ID, please?"

DARBY HAD one more problem. There was no way he was getting his gun through security. He went into the men's room, took his jacket off, and slipped out of the shoulder holster. He draped his jacket over his arm, covering the holster and gun, and found a bank of storage lockers. He stuck the gun and holster into locker 67, slipped the key into his pocket, and went to security.

Darby did not have TSA precheck, so he had to go through the whole aggravating routine. He took off his shoes, his belt, and his jacket, put them in a plastic tray, and sent them through the scanner. He put his watch, his wallet, the change in his pocket, and the key from the storage locker in a little plastic bowl. He stepped into the scanner and held up his arms while the X-ray machine performed its inspection, and the guard on the other side waved him on. He put on his shoes, his belt, and his jacket, and retrieved the items from the plastic bowl. The wallet went in his hip pocket, his key and change in his front pocket.

He slipped on his watch. As always when putting it

on, he checked that the mechanism was working. He pushed the stem sideways, and surreptitiously pulled out the razor-thin wire, just an inch, just enough to make sure it was gliding smoothly.

It was.

All systems were go.

Darby set off looking for his prey.

8.

TEDDY WAS ENJOYING the perks of the priority lounge, in particular the cappuccino he'd managed to coax out of the machine. It had taken some doing. You had to know what buttons to press. Part of the operation was a touch screen and part of it wasn't, and knowing which was which was the key to success. Teddy felt like he did watching kids play video games. A kid would have figured out the machine in a snap. With no kid available, it took Teddy a little longer.

Teddy took a sip of cappuccino, and set it down on the table in front of him. As he glanced up, a man on the other side of the lounge looked away.

In and of itself that was not suspicious, but something about the guy raised a red flag. Perhaps it was that he appeared to have no luggage at all—not even a small bag for a day trip—or just that he looked a little out of place in the exclusive priority lounge.

Could someone be onto him so soon? Apparently someone could. Teddy had no idea who the man was, or how long he'd had been there, but he guessed it had been a while. Surely he couldn't be planning to make his move on the plane? A dead man on a cross-country flight, even if he wasn't discovered until after it landed, would lead to unpleasant inquiries. The assassin—for Teddy suspected that's what he was—would have to make his move now.

DARBY HAD NO intention of getting on the plane. He needed to take care of business before the plane boarded, so he could skip the flight to New York, exit security, and retrieve his gun and holster from the storage locker. So when it came close to the time when the flight would board, he allowed himself to be spotted by his quarry, hoping that would induce the man to do something elusive, to make a move, to try and get away. While that might work with the safety of the security gate to scuttle through, here in the priority lounge there was no place to hide.

It had to be here. And while the authorities would doubtless put together the dead passenger in the priority lounge with the other priority passenger who failed to take the flight, all that meant was the identity on that credit card and ID would have to be retired. It didn't matter. He had several others. In that event, he wondered if the powers that be would decide that L.A. had become too hot and reassign him.

His quarry got up and headed for the buffet table. There wasn't much that time of night, just a few cookies to go along with the coffee from the machine. Before he got there, the man made a quick right turn and headed for the men's room.

Darby gave him a head start and then followed him in.

The priority men's room was small and plush. Two urinals, three sinks, and three toilet stalls. The doors on the stalls were not cheap metal affairs you could see under, but floor-to-ceiling solid wood doors that closed and locked, automatically changing the VACANT sign to OC-CUPIED.

There was no one in the men's room, but one of the stalls read OCCUPIED. The others read VACANT. Darby checked them anyway, just to be safe, but there was no one there. Darby stationed himself in front of the occupied stall. He pressed the stem on his watch and slid out the wire.

A passenger entered the men's room. He saw Darby standing by the occupied stall, and figured he was waiting for it. He saw the vacant signs on the other stalls and frowned. What was wrong with them? He gave Darby a look, and pushed one open. Apparently it met with his approval because he went inside and locked the door.

The *click* of that bolt was followed by the *click* of another; the sign on the door Darby was watching went from OCCUPIED to VACANT. Darby tensed the wire.

The door cracked open, a hand snaked out and yanked him inside. His right arm was snapped in a sudden motion like someone cracking a whip, but his cry of pain was choked off in his throat. It took him a second to realize it was the razor wire, wound around his own neck by the whip-like action and twisted tight as it bit into the flesh. Darby flailed against it, but it was hopeless.

Soon he was beyond realizing anything.

9.

TEDDY FAY RELAXED in his business class seat while the flight attendant refilled his glass of champagne.

"Enjoying your flight, Mr. Barnett?" She gestured to the empty seat next to him. "You certainly have room to spread out, since your friend didn't show."

"I'm traveling alone. I have no idea whose seat that is."

"Would you like his champagne, too?"

"Now you're being naughty," Teddy said.

FAHD CALLED HIS contact in New York. "There's a man named Billy Barnett on the red-eye from L.A."

"Yes?"

"He was supposed to be stopped before he got on the plane. My man has not called in, so I suspect he failed in his objective. I want him met at JFK. See that he doesn't reach Manhattan."

"Of course."

The contact wiped the sleep out of his eyes. It was four AM. He had time, but not much. When did the damn plane land, anyway? He checked the arrival. He had time to send someone to the airport, but who? It would be a routine identification. The passengers all came out the same door, no matter where they were going. His man just had to be standing there. Any moron could do it. He could even give it to Shorty. No, probably not Shorty. How about Cal? It would serve him right. The son of a bitch was getting arrogant. Nothing like a four AM call for a routine job to knock him down a peg. The contact was grinning as he picked up the phone.

TEDDY WOKE UP an hour before the plane would land. He grabbed his kit and went into the restroom. Nothing suspicious in that, many passengers would be taking their toiletries into the lavatories to brush their teeth and freshen up before arrival. But Teddy's wasn't a toiletry kit. It was a makeup kit. He opened it up next to the sink and looked in the mirror. What did he need to change? More specifically, what did he need to change so he wouldn't look like Billy Barnett, but would still look enough like Billy Barnett that the flight attendant wouldn't notice a different passenger in the seat? Hair color, eye color, nose, and chin. He decided to go younger. Darker hair. A paler complexion than a man used to the Hollywood sun. That should do it.

Working quickly, Teddy altered his appearance. He was satisfied with the result. The face looking back from the mirror was unrecognizable from the one before.

Teddy closed up his makeup kit, flushed the toilet,

washed his hands, and peered out the door. The flight attendants were busy getting the breakfast trays ready. Teddy slipped out of the bathroom and returned to his seat. He removed a floppy safari hat from his briefcase, pulled it on, and settled back with his head averted.

The disguise of the disguise worked. The flight attendant served him breakfast without batting an eye.

When they landed, Teddy got off the plane, keeping his head down. As he followed the signs to ground transportation and baggage claim, he pulled the hat off and put it in his briefcase. He didn't want to disguise his appearance now, in fact, attempting to do so would only make others look more closely. He was just another passenger from the flight collecting his bags.

In the baggage claim area, Cal tracked the flight on his iPhone. He knew when the plane set down, long before it was posted on the arrivals board. He didn't know if his quarry had checked baggage, but it didn't matter. All the passengers walked out the same way, whether they were headed for the carousel or for ground transportation.

Cal had the passenger's photo. He checked it again, not that he needed to. He'd checked it when he got the assignment. But four-in-the-morning assignments were a pain in the ass. You weren't at your best when woken from a sound sleep, and in this job you wanted to be at your best.

The target looked like your everyday schmuck, the

type of guy anyone could handle. How the man in L.A. could have missed him was a wonder. It was the only interesting thing about the assignment.

It would be sticky if he couldn't spot him in the airport. He'd have to pull him out of the taxi line. Not good, but doable. It would be worse if the man had a limo waiting, but he probably didn't. In the cluster of limo drivers holding up signs, none said Billy Barnett.

After what seemed an eternity, passengers began to stream out. Some of them headed for the flight's carousel. But not the passenger he wanted.

TEDDY FAY WENT down the ramp and headed for the carousel to retrieve his suitcase. It was among the first bags out, one of the benefits of going business class. He scooped it up and headed for ground transportation.

After his adventure in the LAX airport, Teddy was on guard for trouble here. He easily spotted the hit man standing in line. The man was on high alert, watching all directions. Clearly he was waiting for someone who wasn't expecting him.

Teddy wasn't worried. If the guy hadn't recognized him on his way to the carousel, he wouldn't recognize him now.

Teddy exited the building and got in the taxi line. It was moderately long. He'd have time to make a call before he got in the cab. He popped open his suitcase and took out a burner phone.

10.

MILLIE MARTINDALE WAS having breakfast with Quentin Phillips.

The young agent smiled at her over a forkful of scrambled eggs. "You want to join the FBI?"

"You asked me that last week."

"Yes, I did."

"And what did I say?"

"You said no."

"That's right."

"That's why I'm asking you again."

"You can ask all you like. You're going to get the same answer."

"You loved being in the field. You were good at it."

"I wasn't good handling the press."

"You said 'no comment' as well as anyone."

"I said it to you and you nearly kicked me out of the bedroom."

Circumstances had conspired to send Millie and Quentin on a clandestine assignment together. The fact that she had been the lead and was forced to withhold vital information from him had not set well with the young agent.

Millie smiled, patted him on the hand. "I am never putting myself in that position again."

Millie's cell phone rang. She took it out of her purse.

"Let it go to voice mail," Quentin said.

"It's my other boyfriend. If I don't answer, he'll suspect something."

Quentin smiled. "You're terrible."

Millie clicked the phone on. "Hello?"

"Hello, Millie."

"Who is this?"

"You knew me as Fred Walker."

Millie's face froze. It was the leader of the mission that had caused trouble between Millie and Quentin.

"I'm sorry, I have to take this," Millie said. She got up and stepped away from the table.

Quentin frowned as she went out the door.

"All right, what's up?" Millie demanded.

"I have an assignment for you."

"I don't want it."

"You don't know what it is."

"The last time you gave me an assignment, I got credit for a man you killed."

"No one blamed you. He deserved to die."

"I didn't kill him!" Millie took a breath. "Get someone else."

"Oddly enough, there's no one else I trust. At least for this job. I promise it won't be like last time. You won't have to carry a gun. You won't even have to leave D.C."

"Can I tell Quentin about it?"

"Oh, God, no."

"Then I can't do it."

"A possible terrorist plot is going to succeed or fail based on whether you have a spat with your boyfriend?"

"Why can't you get someone else?"

"There's no one else qualified."

"I find that hard to believe."

"You have the contacts. Your boyfriend doesn't have to know."

"Oh, no? I'm not even sure how to explain this phone call."

"Good. You'll do it. Here's the deal. I just need a go-between. I need you to contact someone for me."

"Why can't you?"

"I'll be out of the country, and he has to be contacted in person. It can't be on the phone, and it can't be in his office. He has to meet you in a neutral setting. That's crucial. Insist on it."

"And if I can get him to do that?"

"Pass along the message and tell him what to do. He'll understand."

"Giving orders was never my forte."

"But you'll do it?"

"I'll do it. Who do you want me to boss around?"

"Lance Cabot."

11.

TEDDY WENT UP the steps and rang the bell.

The door was opened by Fred Flicker. Fred was Stone Barrington's driver, though he was much more than that. A formidable bodyguard, formerly of the Royal Marines, he could handle most men with his bare hands. Teddy was one of the few who did not fall into that category.

"May I help you?"

"Billy Barnett to see Stone Barrington."

"Is he expecting you?"

"We didn't set a specific time, but I'm sure he is."

Fred led Teddy to the outer office where Joan Robertson, Stone Barrington's secretary, sat behind a desk.

Joan looked up. "Yes?"

"This gentleman wishes to see Mr. Barrington."

"And you are?"

"Billy Barnett."

"No, you're not."

Teddy grinned. "Thanks, Joan, you've made my day. Tell Stone that a man you don't recognize claims to be Billy Barnett."

Joan picked up the phone and relayed that message.

Moments later the door opened and Stone Barrington came out. "Where is this imposter?" He sized up Teddy, and grinned. "Oh, I say. Excellent disguise. It would have fooled most people, but not Joan. Fred, take him out and teach him a lesson."

"Not if you want him to keep driving for you," Teddy said.

Stone smiled. "Ah. It is Billy Barnett, after all. Joan, call down to Helene and see if we can rustle him up some breakfast."

"I ate on the plane," Teddy said.

"Coffee and scones, then. And call Dino and tell him he got here. Come in, come in. Leave your suitcase, Fred can take care of it."

Stone ushered Teddy into his study and sat him in an overstuffed leather chair.

"Boy am I glad to see you," Stone said.

"Oh?"

"Dino called. A body was just discovered at LAX with a ticket for the red-eye in his pocket. I didn't recognize the name, but God knows which one you might be using."

"You told Dino I was coming?"

"I invited him to dinner. I hope you don't mind."

"Dino's coming to France?"

"You weren't there when l'Arrington opened. The French gendarmes are much more receptive to police officials than American tourists. So, what happened on the flight?"

"A hit man tried to take me out at LAX, and I'm fairly certain another was waiting for me at JFK."

"Is he alive?"

"The one at JFK is. He was looking for Billy Barnett, not whoever I am now."

"Who are you, by the way?"

Teddy sighed. "Damned if I know."

"And why do you want me to fly you to France?"

"I have my equipment with me. I can't bring it in on a regular flight."

"You don't want to be caught smuggling arms into France."

"That's right."

"You want *me* to smuggle arms into France."

"If you wouldn't mind."

Stone smiled. "You wouldn't tell me anything on the phone. What's this all about?"

"You wouldn't believe it."

12.

FAHD'S NEW YORK contact called him back. "The man you were looking for did not get off the plane. But a passenger with a ticket for the flight was found dead in the men's room in L.A."

"It wasn't him. If it was, my contact in L.A. would have reported in. The person we are looking for is dangerous and elusive. He killed our man in L.A., and he walked away from your man in New York.

"Luckily, we know where he's going. He's going to see someone named Stone Barrington. Send your man to his house, have him follow them when they leave. The man with Stone Barrington will be him."

"Should he take them both out?"

"No. Billy Barnett is dangerous. Just keep tabs on him from a distance. We know they're going to Paris, so check all flights. Let me know as soon as you have something."

Fahd hung up the phone and turned to the new techie, Joram, he had monitoring his computer. Unlike his predecessor, Abad, a stickler who pedantically did everything by the book, Joram was a marshmallow of a man and dutifully did everything he was told. Blind fear of offending made Joram totally trustworthy.

"Get me everything you can on Stone Barrington."

13.

Dino arrived while Stone and Teddy were enjoying coffee and pastries.

"So, this is the man who's been causing all the trouble," Dino said. "Do you want me to put him under arrest?"

"I wish you would," Stone said. "He's been trying to blackmail me into taking him to Paris."

"'Blackmail'?" Teddy said. "I think that's a little harsh."

"He said if I wouldn't take him, he'd turn me in for conspiracy to smuggle arms into the country."

Dino nodded. "Makes sense to me. I guess you'd better go." He sized Teddy up. "And just who might this be?"

"I don't know," Stone said. "I was just trying to figure that out myself. Who are you?"

Teddy shrugged. "I haven't really thought that far ahead."

"Then why the disguise?"

"I figured the opposition would be waiting for me when I landed, so I changed my appearance."

"And your name?"

Teddy smiled. "I hadn't thought of a name. It's not

like you have to show ID to get *off* the plane. I just had to look different. Now I don't know if I should stay with this guise, or switch back to the tried and true."

Dino considers. "Hmm. Young, dumb, and ugly. A good look for you."

"That does it. I'm going with him." Teddy handed Dino his cell phone. "Would you mind taking a photo? I assume Joan has a color printer."

Teddy stood up against a bare wall and Dino snapped a picture.

Teddy held it up for Stone.

"That should do." Stone pressed the intercom. "Joan, I'm sending you a photo. I need six color copies, passport size. Thanks."

"Right away," Joan said.

"So what's this all about?" Dino said. "I've been pumping Stone for information, and he doesn't know anything."

"I didn't want to talk on the phone," Teddy said. "I was afraid my phone might be compromised. Turns out I was justified. Yesterday I got a phone call from Lance Cabot."

Dino raised his eyebrows. "Lance Cabot, the director of the CIA? Lance Cabot, who put you on the top of his Most Wanted list and turned the bureau upside down trying to catch you?"

"The very one."

"I thought he subscribed to the theory that you were dead."

"That's a folk myth. He might have wished it, but he never really bought it."

"Then out of the blue he calls you up and says he knows who you are?"

"Actually, my name was never mentioned. He called me Billy Barnett."

"He implied he knew who Billy Barnett was?"

"He more than implied it—he acted on that assumption. He told me there's a mole in the CIA station in Paris, and he wants me to remove it."

"Why would there be a mole in Paris?"

"He has no idea. But the fact that there might be is cause for alarm. Enough for him to admit my existence."

"You say he called yesterday?" Dino asked.

"Yes."

"And people are already trying to kill you?"

"Yes. His phone must be tapped. It has to be a little embarrassing for the head of the CIA."

"Did you tell him?"

"Well, I can't call him. But don't worry, I'm taking care of it."

14.

LANCE CABOT SAT at his desk going over the personnel files of some of his senior agents. A station head at the Chicago bureau was stepping down, and he needed to find a replacement. There was no one available with the necessary qualifications and experience. Someone would have to be promoted, it was just a question of finding the right agent. Excellence in the field did not necessarily translate into leadership abilities. Of necessity, some of the best agents worked alone.

Lance frowned, tossed a file on his desk, and reached for another.

The phone rang. Lance scooped it up. "Yes?"

It was Claire, his secretary. "There's a Miss Millie Martindale here to see you."

"Who?"

"Millie Martindale. She says you worked together."

"Oh." Lance remembered vaguely. Millie Martindale was the girlfriend of an FBI agent, and had actually been involved in resolving a mission involving the kidnapping of a congressman's daughter. But why she thought that qualified her to show up at the CIA director's office without an appointment was beyond him. He'd read her the riot act. "All right. Send her in."

Millie Martindale came through the door as if they were long-lost friends. "Lance, how are you? It's been too long. We have so much catching up to do. Listen, I have another appointment. Could you walk with me, and we can talk along the way?"

Lance stared at her, dumbfounded. He blinked twice and then found his voice. "Now, Miss Martindale . . ."

"I know, I know, I should have called. You have a very important job, and I don't want to interrupt it. But I do need to talk to you and you need to talk to me, so if you would walk me out."

Millie had linked her arm in Lance's and was literally pulling him toward the door.

"I have no intention—"

"You can buy me a strawberry milk shake."

Lance's mouth fell open. He said nothing, but allowed himself be pulled toward the door.

In the outer office, Claire glanced up inquiringly.

"The director's going out," Millie said. "Hold his calls."

They left the office, walked down the hall, and waited silently together in the elevator. Neither said a word until they were outside.

"Where did you learn that?" Lance demanded.

"What?"

" 'Strawberry milk shake.' "

"A mutual friend. He said not to use it unless I had to."

"What the devil is going on?"

"Your security has been compromised. I don't know if your office has been bugged, but your phone has been hacked."

"Where'd you get that idea?"

"You just gave our mutual friend an assignment. Someone tried to kill him on his way to New York. He sent me to warn you your phone must be hacked."

"How does he know it's not his phone?"

"With all due respect, sir, and please understand that it's him speaking—"

"Yes?"

"He says you're stupid for asking the question. He says you're careless for letting your phone be hacked. He says you sent him on a mission that's compromised from the get-go."

"He's not going to do it?"

"He'll still do it, but he says you owe him double."

Lance smiled. "Typical."

"What are you paying him?"

"Nothing."

"That's what I figured. Anyway, he says you can talk to me. You're sending him to Paris to ferret out a mole. He's not going to be able to call you for obvious reasons. He doesn't want this going though Agency channels. I'll be your go-between. He says he's going out on a limb, and he wants you to have his back. It may be crucial for him to get in touch with you at once. If I call your office, put me though immediately. I'm not going to talk on the phone. I'll tell you where to meet me, and you drop every-thing and go."

"That's going to be damn annoying."

"If you can't do it, let me know, and he'll come home."

"What?"

"He'll bail on the operation. He's says this is either important to you or it isn't. If it's important enough for him to pull up stakes and rush off to Paris, it's important enough for you to take a phone call. Immediately. No red tape. If I call your office, your secretary puts me through. You have to make that clear. I'm a high-priority confidential source, and my calls take precedence over anything. You can be in the middle of a meeting with your station chiefs, and you don't say take a number I'll call back, you pick up the phone. And when I give you a location you say something's come up I've got to go, and you head there. The first time that doesn't happen, our friend will be booking his airfare home."

"I can't believe you're talking to me like this."

"I'm not talking to you like this. *He's* talking to you like this. It's not going to do you any good to get angry at me. If you fail to comply with his wishes, I will merely relay the information and he'll take it from there. But I suggest that you don't put him in that position. I'm merely telling you what will happen if you do.

"If all that is agreeable to you—bad choice of words, I'm sure it isn't—but if not, tell me now and you can start grooming someone else for the job. Are we agreed?"

"I guess we have to be."

"Good." Millie smiled. "Our friend has no messages this time. When you get back to the office, check out your phones."

Millie turned and walked away.

Lance didn't go back to his office. He walked down by the river, sat on a secluded bench, and took his cell phone apart.

It didn't take long to find it. A small microchip hidden by the battery. He pried it out, and looked around to see that no one was watching. He smashed his cell phone on a rock, and threw it in the Potomac.

Lance was pretty angry.

He got a lot on the throw.

15.

JORAM GLANCED UP from the computer. "A line went dead."

"Which one?" Fahd said.

"Lance Cabot."

"Shit! When you say dead, you don't mean the phone's just been turned off?"

"No, sir. Either the battery has been removed or the line has been disconnected. It could come on again, but we have no way of knowing if or when."

"What about the other one?"

"Billy Barnett? That line is still open, but inactive. There have been no calls on it since yesterday."

Fahd was frustrated—it seemed as if his primary sources of vital information might be drying up.

"Did you get anything else on Stone Barrington?"

"Yes, sir. The man has so many interests that more information is coming in all the time. He is a lawyer with many irons in the fire. He is a partner with Woodman & Weld, yet he operates alone out of his own town house. He is also a member of a five-man group of lawyers who handle a few elite clients, including the President of the United States."

"Really?"

"He owns several houses, including an English country manor, and is the owner or co-owner of a string of high-end hotels. He also owns and flies his own jet plane."

"What kind?"

"I'm researching that now. But he keeps it at the air-field in Teterboro, New Jersey."

Fahd snatched up the phone and called his contact in New York. "Is your man staking out Stone Barrington's house?"

"Yes, he is. So far there's been no movement."

"Stone Barrington owns a jet. It's at Teterboro air-port. Keep monitoring flight reservations, but be advised our quarry may head for Teterboro."

"Do you want him stopped there?"

"No, just confirm the takeoff. We'll pick him up in Paris."

Fahd slammed down the phone and turned to the techie at the computer. "Still dead?"

Joram, wearing headphones, wasn't sure what he'd been asked. It barely registered that Fahd was talking to him. "Sir?"

"Lance Cabot's line. Is it still dead?"

"Yes, sir."

Fahd snatched up the phone again and called his con-tact in D.C. "We have a problem with your agent."

"What about her?"

"I think her cover may be blown."

16.

LANCE LIKED WENDY. They'd met at a fund-raiser for Congressman Wilkerson, and she'd been so casual. Not pushing an agenda, like everyone else in Washington. Not impressed by his position, but not scared off. Her response, "Oh, is that an interesting job?" had been so beautifully understated they both wound up laughing at it.

He'd walked her home. Her apartment wasn't that far from the party. She told him about her job, as a secretary, as if it wasn't something to apologize for, or merely a rung up the corporate ladder. She was happy being a secretary, she found it a perfectly meaningful line of work.

He'd been seeing her for six months.

He didn't call her now, probably wouldn't have, even if he'd *had* a phone. Instead he walked to her apartment, just as he'd done so many times before, though not usually during the day.

Wendy lived in a small third-floor walk-up. It was a railroad flat, actually, though Lance never thought of it that way. Her bedroom was cozy, intimate. He liked it, though he never stayed the night. He didn't want to go from there to work in the morning.

Lance went up to the third floor and knocked. He didn't expect a response. She would be at work.

She'd given him a key, though he'd never used it. He felt guilty using it now, but he had to do it. Someone had bugged his phone, and he had to find out who. Wendy was, regrettably, a person of interest. She'd had opportunity. She could have taken his phone apart while he was in the shower and inserted the chip.

Lance didn't want to think it was possible. Not Wendy. Not her. And yet he had to go into her apartment when she wasn't there and search through her belongings, violating her privacy and betraying her trust, to try to find the least little thing to incriminate her.

Lance felt guilty as he opened the door.

Until he saw the apartment had been cleared out.

17.

TEDDY WATCHED OUT the back window as Fred Flicker drove him out of Stone Barrington's garage. A gray Lexus pulled away from the curb and fell in behind them.

"Fred, we're being followed. Can you take care of that?"

"Do you care if he knows that we're doing it?"

"I'd prefer that he didn't, but sometimes it can't be helped."

"It usually can," Fred said. He squeezed by a bus, hit the corner, and swung a left turn just as the light was changing, leaving the other car trapped in a snarl of traffic.

"Nicely done," Teddy said. "Now I can get a new cell phone. Drop me at the shop and cruise around until I call you on it."

Fred dropped Teddy off and sped away, just in case the man he ditched was looking for his car.

The clerk in the cell phone store was confused.

"You want to upgrade your system?"

"No, I just want another phone."

"But this phone works."

"Yes, it does. I want to transfer the data on it to another phone. Can you do that?"

"Of course, I can. But to what phone?"

"The one I buy."

"What kind of phone do you want to buy?"

"One that does the same thing this does."

"You want to buy the same phone?"

"If you've got it."

"We have a newer version. Your phone is quite old."

"The newer version would work the same way this one does?"

"More or less."

"What's the less?"

"It would have more features."

"Would it have *these* features?"

"Yes, among others."

"Fine. I'll take it."

"So, you want an upgrade."

Teddy sighed. "You win. I want an upgrade. Can you do it?"

"Of course."

"Fine. Transfer the data. Except for the number."

"Sir?"

"I want a new phone number."

"You know there are serious drawbacks to having a new number."

"Such as?"

"People won't be able to call you."

Teddy smiled. "I certainly hope not."

———

JORAM HATED TO be the bearer of bad news. He had a wife and two small children. All he cared about was keeping his head down. Then he wound up in Fahd's office, monitoring important calls.

"Now the other phone's dead," Joram said. He sounded like he was apologizing.

"Billy Barnett?"

"Yes."

"They're both dead?"

"Yes."

"But they could be activated again?"

"It's possible."

"Fine. Then you're done for the time being. You can go back to your post in the other room."

Joram struggled to keep the relief from showing on his face. "Yes, sir."

Fahd stopped him. "But first, whose lines have you been monitoring?"

"Lance Cabot and Billy Barnett."

Fahd grimaced. "I'm afraid your memory is faulty. Whose lines are these again?"

Joram looked terrified. He gawked at Fahd stupidly, trying to divine the right answer. "I don't remember?"

Fahd smiled. "Yes, I didn't think you did. Good man. So you won't be mentioning any names to anyone. Am I right?"

"Yes, sir. Absolutely," Joram said.

It took all he could do not to run out of the room.

18.

FRED DROVE DOWN the block and turned into Stone Barrington's underground garage.

"The car that was following us is on the corner," Fred said. "He must have come back here when I lost him. What do you want to do about it?"

"At the moment, nothing," Teddy said.

"I'm not comfortable having someone watching the house."

"It's just until we leave for the airport."

"Am I driving you to the airport?"

"Teterboro. Stone, Dino, and I are going to France."

On his way in, Joan presented Teddy with six color prints of the passport photos. "Will these do?"

"Perfect," Teddy said. "Thanks, Joan."

Teddy and Fred went on into Stone's study.

Stone and Dino were drinking Knob Creek. "Good, you're back. Care for a drink? You, too, Fred?"

"I just wanted to report. We were followed by a man in a gray Lexus. He's currently parked on the corner of your block."

"I see," Stone said. He turned to Teddy. "What do you want to do about it?"

"It's probably better he doesn't know we spotted him," Teddy said. "If he's still hanging around after we leave, Fred, feel free to beat him to a pulp."

Stone saw the photos in Teddy's hand. "How did the picture come out?"

Teddy smiled. "I think it's some of Dino's best work."

"Fuck you," Dino said.

"What are you going to do with it?" Stone said. "I don't have the equipment to mock up credentials."

"It's okay. I'll use an old one. Where's my suitcase?"

"I'll get it for you," Fred said. He was back in minutes with the suitcase.

Teddy unlocked it, and took out a bulging leather zip pouch slightly larger than a wallet. He unzipped it and began leafing through IDs. There were credit cards, driver's licenses, and various credentials.

"Ah, here we are," Teddy said. "CIA credentials. What don't I need anymore? Oh, here we go. Felix Dressler. Look at those sideburns. Major pain in the ass to put on. But, shave them off and he'd look like me. At least he'd look like me in that passport photo. Which means I can use these credentials. Gentlemen, meet Agent Felix Dressler, on a longtime covert assignment just emerging from deep cover."

"What assignment?"

"I'll come up with something."

"So, what's his story?" Dino said.

"I suppose he ought to have one," Teddy said. "Can I get on the Internet?"

"Be my guest," Stone said.

Teddy sat down at Stone's computer, hacked into the CIA site, and posted the credentials of Felix Dressler, establishing him as a longtime agent, the veteran of several clandestine missions. He designated a large portion of Dressler's file as classified, eyes-only material, that could only be accessed by senior officers with top-priority clearance.

"That'll do for now," Teddy said. "I'll make up more background on the plane."

FAHD GOT THE info on the plane from Joram and called his contact in New York. "Stone Barrington's private jet is a Citation CJ3-Plus. If they head for Teterboro Airport, then that is the plane they will be taking. Tell your man to get the tail numbers and trace the flight plan. I'm told the jet does not have the range to fly to Paris nonstop. Find out where they plan to refuel on the way."

"Do you want them intercepted at one of those stops?"

"If the opportunity arises where you have someone already in place, but it will probably be impossible. This is a tricky individual. I would like some assurance he didn't get off the plane."

"I understand. It will be done."

"See that it is. So far your employees have proven to be utterly inept. If I am disappointed again, I will hold you personally responsible."

19.

Stone Barrington laid in a flight plan, guided his Citation CJ3+ down the runway, and took off.

In the back of the luxurious jet, Teddy looked across the Hudson at the receding New York City skyline. "How long's the flight?"

"About an hour," Dino said.

"Huh?"

Dino grinned. "We're going to D.C."

"Oh?"

"This is a nice plane, but it can't fly nonstop to Paris. We're trading up."

"For what?"

"You'll see."

"It better not be a CIA plane. That would not be funny."

"Never fear. No one even knows you're going. The plane's for me and Stone."

"Who's providing it?"

Dino grinned. "Viv. One of the perks of being married to a company bigwig."

Dino's wife was the chief operating officer for

Strategic Services, the second-largest security agency in the country. They maintained a number of aircraft capable of international flights.

An hour later Stone set down at Dulles International Airport, and they emerged from the plane to see a familiar figure walking down the runway.

"Mike," Dino said. "What are you doing here?"

Mike Freeman, the head of Strategic Services, operated from his office in New York City, so his appearance in D.C. was a surprise.

"I had a meeting with a few select clients. Politicians who like to feel important. They don't really need protection, but it strokes their egos to have it."

"And to be seen having lunch with the CEO of Strategic Services."

"Exactly," Mike said. "You wouldn't believe how many people were called over to our table for an introduction. Anyway, I was in town, and I heard a rumor one of our executives was abusing her privileges by flying her husband around in company aircraft, so I thought I'd check it out."

"I'm afraid you've been misled," Dino said. "She's not flying *me* around. Stone batted his eyes at her, and she can't deny him anything."

Mike turned to Teddy. "I won't ask who this is. I'm sure the answer would be less than illuminating."

Mike had offered Teddy a job once, anytime Teddy wanted to take it. The offer was still standing.

"Good to see you, too, Mike," Teddy said.

Mike dropped the bantering tone and said, "Is this anything you might need a little help with?"

"I appreciate the offer, Mike, but at the moment, I have no idea," Teddy said.

Mike nodded. "Viv was a little vague on details. How long do you need the plane for?"

"It's open-ended," Teddy said. "We're going for a joyride, and we'll be back when the thrill wears off."

"Sounds like just the type of deal I'd like to get one of my best aircraft involved in. Seriously, though, if you need help, whistle."

"Thanks," Teddy said.

Mike walked them to the plane. The huge Gulfstream G650 was indeed imposing. "It's not as luxurious as Air Force One, but I hope it will do. I also have to apologize for making you come all the way down here to get it. It flew in from England this morning carrying a couple of diplomats, and they might have been grumpy if we tried to divert them to New York. Anyway, I hope it will be to your liking."

"I think I've flown it before," Stone said.

"Yes. That was a business trip when Viv actually had a legitimate reason to go to Paris and you got to tag along. I believe this will be its first actual joyride. Anyway, it should be wheels up in half an hour." Mike put up his hands. "Look, I know you like to fly, Stone, but if you don't mind, our flight crew will handle this one. Insurance purposes, you understand. If *you* were to drop it in the drink, we wouldn't be covered."

Stone snorted.

"Anything else I can do for you?" Mike said ironically.

"Does this hunk of junk have Internet service?" Teddy said.

"Not if you're planning on committing a felony."

"Forget I asked."

20.

FAHD SNAPPED INTO the phone, "They what!"

"Flew to Dulles Airport in Washington, D.C. They'd landed before we even confirmed the flight plan."

"What's their next stop?"

"We don't know. Stone Barrington has submitted no further flight plan. We're looking, but we can't find it."

"I suppose a man with his amount of money could bribe someone to keep it off the books."

"He can't take off without filing a flight plan. It isn't safe for other aircraft."

"Is the plane still there?"

"We have men on the way to the airport. Confirming a flight didn't take off isn't as easy as confirming one did."

"It's a diversion. They knew we would be checking reservations at JFK, so they flew to Dulles. Check reservations on every plane leaving Dulles for France for the names Stone Barrington, Dino Bacchetti, and Billy Barnett."

Fahd slammed the phone down, went to the door, and bellowed, "Joram!"

The techie looked up from his computer. "Yes, sir?"

"Get in here."

Joram swallowed hard, got up, and went into the other room, wondering what he could possibly have done wrong.

"Sit at that computer. I need you to find some information, and I don't want to keep yelling for you."

"Yes, sir. What do you need, sir?"

"Find out where Stone Barrington stays when he goes to Paris."

Joram looked up the question on the Internet. The answer came back almost immediately.

"Sir?"

"Yes?"

"Stone Barrington owns a house in Paris. He bought it fairly recently. It's a modest house, but quite large enough to accommodate his friends."

"Excellent," Fahd said. He called Glenville, an independent agent he used sometimes in Paris. Glenville would have more flexibility than his other main contact in Paris, a carefully placed mole in the CIA office. "A man named Billy Barnett is en route to Paris. We've lost him along the way, but he's traveling with two men: Stone Barrington and Police Commissioner Dino Bacchetti. Stone Barrington owns a house in town. Intercept Barnett there, and follow him wherever he goes. Don't let him know he's being followed, but don't let him out of your sight. Let me know when you have him, and I'll send further instructions."

21.

"YOU REALIZE I can't stay at your house," Teddy said.

Teddy, Stone, and Dino were having a cocktail served by an attractive flight attendant.

"I'll try not to take it personally," Stone said. "Why not?"

"Isn't it a safe house you bought from the CIA?"

"Actually, it is."

"Any connection to the CIA is bad for me."

"Why? You're doing work for them. You're *supposed* to be an agent."

"Not one who's hanging out in a CIA safe house owned by a billionaire. That's a dead giveaway."

"If Lance's phone was bugged and people are already trying to kill you, that ship has sailed."

"That's true." Teddy paused. "Which makes this a suicide mission. I'm looking for a mole in the Agency, and the mole already knows I'm coming."

"Exactly. So why even continue with this plan?"

"It's risky, but I think it will still work. The other agents won't know the truth. Since I don't know who's the mole, I have to keep up the pretense for everyone. If I do it well, the agent who's not buying it will be the mole."

"That's your plan?" Dino said.

"I haven't come up with a plan. At the moment, all I'm concerned with is not getting killed. Anyway, I can't stay at the safe house. It's not safe."

"So what do you plan to do?"

"I'm going to rent an apartment that a spy on the run might afford. Actually, I can use a little help with that. Stone, you have some experience buying real estate. Do you mind a little intrigue?"

"I wouldn't mind a little myself," Dino said.

"Do you need an apartment immediately?" Stone said.

"Unless you've got a better idea. I don't want to sleep on the street."

"How about l'Arrington?" The Paris branch of the Arrington Hotels, named after Stone's late wife, was one of the finest in the city. "What do you say we check in there for one night? The next day you can rent your apartment, and Dino and I will move into my house."

"Works for me," Teddy said.

"Great. I'll call them and get the Royal Suite."

"Can you get it on such short notice?" Teddy said.

"Hey," Stone said. "I own the place."

"Yeah," Dino said sardonically. "And he busts *my* chops about Peter Luger."

22.

JORAM JUMPED OUT of his chair. "Sir!"

Fahd looked up from this desk. He was clearly annoyed. "Yes?"

"Stone Barrington's not going to his home."

"What?"

"He's not going to the address I gave you. He just made a reservation at l'Arrington Hotel."

"What!"

"Yes, sir."

"He's staying at the l'Arrington?"

Joram didn't point out that Fahd's use of the word *the* was redundant. The French *l'*, meaning *the*, took care of it. "Yes, sir. The reservation just appeared, for a party of three."

"Damn!"

"Sir?"

"Why is he staying at the l'Arrington? He has a perfectly good house."

"He also owns the hotel, sir."

"Oh?"

"Half of it, anyway. A Frenchman named Marcel Du-Bois is the co-owner."

"He's going to stay there the whole time he's in Paris?"

"That's hard to say, sir."

"Well, how long is his reservation for?"

"Just for one night."

Fahd gave him the evil eye. "You could have said that to begin with." Fahd snatched up the phone and called Glenville back. "He's going to the l'Arrington."

"Sir?"

"The l'Arrington Hotel. Pick him up there."

"He's not going to his house?"

"Not today. He's checking in at the hotel."

"Do you have any idea when?"

"No, but you'll know it when it happens. Stone Barrington owns half the hotel. His reservation includes Dino Bacchetti and Billy Barnett. I assume you have located a photo of Barnett?"

"Of course."

"He may look different. Our man in New York never spotted him. Do you have photos of Stone Barrington and Dino Bacchetti?"

"Yes."

"He'll be with them."

"LET ME OUT here," Teddy said.

The car service was en route from the airport to the hotel.

"You're not going to the hotel?" Stone said.

"If you wouldn't mind checking in for me, I have an errand to run."

Dino snorted. "Well, that could cover any act in the penal code."

"Will you be back in time for dinner?" Stone said.

"Oh, yes. It shouldn't take long."

Teddy hopped out at the corner and strolled down the street. It was a ten-minute walk to a small antique shop that featured jewelry and knickknacks. The owner was a diminutive Frenchman with a graying moustache.

Teddy stepped inside and flipped Felix Dressler's new CIA credentials open on the counter.

The owner took a look and cocked his head. "Who are you?"

Teddy pointed to the credentials.

The owner made a face. "Please. Do you expect me to be impressed by an amateurish set of phony credentials?"

Teddy smiled. "That's hurtful, André."

Andre frowned. "Do I know you?"

Teddy smiled. "Under another name."

"What name?"

"Any name you like."

André blinked. "Teddy?"

Teddy put up his hand. "Whoa, whoa. I don't know this man of whom you speak. But let's assume an acquaintance and take it from there. Can you do the work?"

"You want more CIA credentials?"

"Passports, actually. Six of them, in six different names. All with this photo." Teddy laid the six passport photos on the counter. "Can that be done?"

André squinted at him shrewdly. "If the price is right."

"Name it."

After a short negotiation, Teddy and André agreed on a price.

"When do you need these?"

"First thing tomorrow morning."

"A rush order. You didn't say that."

"You can't do it?"

"It will affect the price."

After another round of bargaining, they were agreed.

23.

THOUGH GLENVILLE WAS used to a bit of unpredictability on the job, this mission was a bit of a mess. First he was told to stake out Stone Barrington's house to pick up Billy Barnett, and it turned out nobody was going there.

Then he was told Barnett was checking into l'Arrington with his friends, and the other two show up without him. Glenville had no trouble identifying Stone Barrington and Dino Bacchetti from their photos, but Billy Barnett was not with them. They checked in for him and had his luggage sent up to his room.

Only it wasn't a room with a number, something he could stake out and monitor when the man arrived. No, all three men were in the extensive Royal Suite, which in addition to the main suite, had smaller connecting suites for members of the entourage. So Billy Barnett wouldn't have to go to the front desk like he would if he had his own room, he could go straight up to the Royal Suite and knock on the door.

With that in mind, Glenville had taken the elevator up

to the floor with the Royal Suite, only to find a man who was obviously a hotel detective lurking in the hall.

So Glenville was hanging out in the lobby, keeping an eye on the front desk, in case anyone asked for a key to the Royal Suite, and an eye on the elevator, in case anyone vaguely resembling his photo of Billy Barnett came in and got on.

It was not a great plan. Glenville figured he'd probably miss Barnett going in, but if the three men went out together he'd have him. It wasn't perfect, but he couldn't think of anything better.

He reminded himself to snap a picture, if by a miracle the man ever did appear.

24.

TEDDY SHOWED UP in a beret.

Stone and Dino were having drinks on the balcony when the bell to the suite rang. Dino went to the door, looked through the peephole, and opened the door.

Dino surveyed Teddy critically. "I'm not sure it suits you," he said.

"It would if I changed my appearance, but then I wouldn't match my credentials." Teddy took off the beret, and spun it like a Frisbee in the direction of the couch. "Ah, Paris in the springtime," he said.

"Brings back memories?"

"Yes, and none of them good. 'Look, honey, there's the café where I killed the German courier.'"

"Did you accomplish your purpose, whatever it was?" Stone said.

"I stretched my legs. That was the main thing. Where's my suitcase?"

"In your bedroom. Don't worry, it hasn't been

touched. I don't think Houdini could get through that lock you have on it."

"Even so, I'd feel better not leaving it lying around in the room."

"I could have the hotel lock it up for you in the safe," Stone said, "but that would call attention to it."

"Not if you tell them it's yours. Put it in your room and change the luggage tag. You're Mr. Big Hotel Owner, they'll rent out Fort Knox for you."

"Fine. Let's get it."

Stone and Dino showed Teddy to his room. His mini-suite could have passed for the Presidential Suite in most hotels.

Teddy's suitcase was in the middle of his bedroom. The lock was clearly undisturbed. He hefted the heavy case onto the bed and punched in a code. Then he put his key in the lock. The sequence was important. Without the code, the key would not even fit. He turned the key a quarter turn, punched in a second code, and turned the key the rest of the way. He punched in a third code, opened the suitcase, and unpacked his clothes.

Next he took out a clear-plastic zippered case, crammed with packets of hundred-dollar bills. Teddy put the case in the room safe. Not that Teddy trusted the safe, but it was only cash. A good deal of cash, but even so.

Last, Teddy unzipped his heavy-duty equipment bag. He selected a spare burner phone, and a gun and shoulder holster.

He left his state-of-the-art, personally designed sniper

rifle in the bag. He had no use for it as yet, and he felt better having it under lock and key.

He slipped on the shoulder holster, closed the suitcase, and went through the ritual of locking it again.

When he was done he dragged the suitcase to the front door. Stone was standing there with a luggage tag.

"Take your tag off and hang on to it," Stone said. "I know you don't want your tag on my case when I take it to my house."

"Not exactly the back trail I care to leave," Teddy said.

A bellboy came up to retrieve the suitcase. He had a hotel security guard with him.

"Excellent," Stone said. "I need this locked up overnight."

"Yes, sir."

Stone slipped the bellboy a bill. The security guard regarded the money enviously. Stone smiled slightly and slipped him a bill, too.

"Was that necessary?" Teddy said, as the men took the suitcase to the elevator.

"What?"

"Tipping the guard?"

"It wasn't necessary, but when someone tries to take the suitcase away from him, I'd like him on my side."

"Well, now I need to get a suitcase," Teddy said.

"What for?"

"To put my clothes in."

"I could have them sent on."

"That would be messy. And I need the suitcase as a prop. I'll pick one up on our way back from dinner."

"Will anything be open that late?"

"Someone will have a suitcase." Teddy smiled. "Luckily, it doesn't matter what it looks like."

25.

THEY DINED AT L'Abeille at the Hotel Shangri-La,
a posh restaurant where dinner clothes were preferred and price was no consideration. At least it wasn't
to Teddy and Dino. Stone was paying.

There was a waiting list for L'Abeille. Dino might
have made more of the fact that Stone was able to get a
reservation, had he not been distracted by the name of
the restaurant. In keeping with its lush garden view,
abeille meant "bee."

"I know it's the only reason we're here," Dino said.
"You have it in your mind that *B* is for *Barrington*. Like,
it's your own personal restaurant."

"*B* is also for *Bacchetti*," Stone pointed out.

"Did I make the reservation? Did I order frog legs?
Which are surprisingly good, by the way. Did I choose a
place where I have to wear this monkey suit? I don't dress
this well for the mayor's dinner."

Stone laughed. "Can you find him something to do
on this trip, Billy? He's really cranky."

Teddy grinned and dug into his escargot. "Enjoy the
ride, Dino. This may be the last meal we have together

for a while. Then you'll be stuck with Stone. And, knowing him, he'll snag an attractive young dinner date, and you'll be on your own."

Stone said, "You're not helping."

"Okay, Dino," Teddy said. "I've got a job for you, and it's not going to be easy. Are you up for it?"

"Sure."

"You know there's a man watching us."

Dino's raised his eyebrows. "What?"

"He picked us up when we left the hotel and followed us here. He's out there sulking on the sidewalk while we're living the high life in here."

"Do you want me to have him arrested? I could call the prefect of police, and he'd be glad to oblige."

"I'm sure you could. I'm afraid it's a little harder than that."

"You want me to ID him without him knowing it? It's a lot harder if I can't arrest him."

"I can imagine. No, not that."

"So, what's this really hard thing you want me to do?"

"When we leave here, and he follows us . . ."

"Yes?"

"Pretend you don't see him."

26.

THE NEXT MORNING, Teddy woke up, showered, shaved, and left the hotel. His shadow was waiting for him across the street. Teddy smiled to himself. He hailed a cab and took it to a little bistro down by the Seine. It was a place, Teddy recalled, where it was hard to get a cab. One usually had to call for them.

Teddy paid the cab off and went inside. The café was crowded at breakfast time. He tipped the waiter for a table with a river view. It was an unnecessary gesture. All tables had a river view.

Teddy allowed himself to be seated and ordered coffee. Out of the corner of his eye he could see his shadow accepting a table on the other side of the room.

Teddy's coffee came. He took a sip, leaned back, and enjoyed the view. He was about to take another sip when he reacted, set the coffee down, and pulled out the burner phone he'd equipped himself with, and pretended to answer a call.

"Yes? . . . Now?" He sighed. "Very well."

Teddy stuck the burner phone back in his pocket. He

stood up, took a sip of coffee, apologetically palmed the waiter a bill, and went out the door.

The taxi he'd tipped handsomely to wait for him was down the block. On seeing him, it drove in his direction. Teddy stepped out in the street and raised his hand, as if hailing it by chance. He hopped in, and the taxi took off. Out the back window he could see his shadow coming out the restaurant door.

TEDDY GOT OUT three blocks away, made sure no one was following him, and went into the antique shop.

André was behind the counter enjoying an espresso and a scone.

"Taking a break, André?" Teddy said. "I hope that means you're done."

"Of course I'm done. When have I ever not been done? I do what I say."

André moved his expresso aside and put the passports on the counter.

"How do they look?" Teddy said.

André shrugged. "There's nothing I can do about the ugly man in the photo, but they'll get you in and out of the country."

Teddy picked up a passport and flipped it open. It was for Arnold Mycroft. He flipped open another one. It was an equally convincing forgery for Daniel Remington. He looked at the other passports, just for show, but they were perfect. He'd known they would be.

"Great," Teddy said. "I believe we're all square, then."

André coughed apologetically. "I realize you are kidding. Anyone else I would have to kill. There is a balance, as you well know."

"And well deserved," Teddy said, handing over a roll of cash.

"Will I see you again on this trip?" André said.

"Don't take this personally, but I hope not."

"I understand."

TEDDY CAME OUT of the shop. Once again, he made sure he was alone. He hailed a taxi and took it to the Gare de Lyon railway station. He made his way around the tracks on the main level, and took the stairs to the concourse below. The bank of long-term lockers was right where he remembered. He rented six of them, one right after another. In each he put a passport and ten thousand dollars in cash. He took the six keys, left the station, hailed a cab, and returned to l'Arrington.

The shadow was waiting for him. He was inconspicuous, but not to a man of Teddy's talent. It was all Teddy could do not to wave to him.

27.

TEDDY JOINED HIS friends in the hotel dining room for breakfast.

"Okay," Teddy said. "Here's the plan."

He was wasting his breath. At the moment, Dino's plan involved getting a second helping of crêpe suzette. Stone's plan involved making his way through every English-language newspaper available at the hotel.

Teddy smiled indulgently, then went and stood in line for his own individually prepared, made-to-order omelet. He opted for scallions and peppers. Returning to the table, he applauded his choice.

Finishing his omelet, he pushed his plate back with an air of finality. "Okay," he said, "it's time for me to check in with the CIA. That should be interesting. They won't be expecting me. Except for the mole, of course."

"Who is the station head?" Stone said.

"A guy named Norton. I don't know him, which is good. He doesn't know me, either, but he's going to hate me a lot."

"What for?" Dino asked.

"Aside from just on general principles: for pulling

rank, giving orders, and not letting him into the loop. He'll fall all over himself to cooperate with me while hoping I get hit by a truck."

"What's your cover story?" Dino asked.

"Sorry, that's above your pay grade."

"Is that what you're going to tell *him*?"

"See why he'll hate me a lot? I have no cover story, and it saves me having to make one up. And because my identity is marked as top secret in the system, he won't be able to call my bluff or do anything about it."

Teddy passed over a fat envelope. "Okay, Dino, you're up. Here's some Monopoly money, a burner phone, and a list of what I need. You're renting an apartment in the name of Fenton Towne."

"Should I claim to be Fenton Towne?"

"Certainly not. You're Fenton Towne's manservant."

"Fuck you, too." Dino grinned. "You're loving this, aren't you?"

"Welcome to the world of espionage. A lot of espionage is hiding in plain sight. I'm going to do what I have to do, and my tail is going to know some of it—and some of it he's not. Controlling what he knows, doling out only the information I want him to have, gives me the upper hand."

Dino grumbled good-naturedly. "I thought this spy stuff would be a little more exciting."

"Don't worry. I'll get you some action."

TEDDY WENT UP to the suite and packed his clothes in the secondhand suitcase he'd bought the night before.

He called the front desk and had a bellboy take the suitcase down and get him a cab. As he climbed in, he spotted his shadow watching.

Teddy had the cab take him in the opposite direction from the apartment he'd rented over the phone the night before. After about a mile, he had the driver pull over and let him out. He stood on the street corner with his suitcase for a few minutes, then hailed a cab going the other way. He got out three blocks from his apartment and walked the rest of the way. The suitcase wasn't heavy. It held only his clothes, and not all of them at that.

The super who lived in the basement apartment had his keys, as promised. He surrendered them gladly, impressed with Teddy's CIA credentials.

The apartment was what Teddy expected. A kitchen the size of a closet, a small living room, and a bedroom not much bigger. Teddy didn't mind. It was perfect for his purpose.

Teddy flopped his suitcase on the bed and unpacked. It didn't take long. He put his toiletries in the bathroom, hung up his jacket, and put his clothes in the dresser. When he was done, he closed the suitcase and stashed it under the bed.

He locked the apartment, went out, and hailed a cab. As expected, his shadow was right on his tail.

28.

GLENVILLE REPORTED IN. "This morning Billy Barnett checked out of the hotel and moved his things into an apartment. I followed him there and got his address." Glenville didn't mention losing him at the café. Indeed, his main reason for calling about the apartment was to head off any inquiry into what he'd done earlier in the day.

"He's there now?" Fahd said.

"No, sir. He came right back out and went straight to the U.S. Embassy."

"He's there now?"

"Yes. So he is who we thought he was."

"Good. Then our mole can take over. Back off and let things develop. I can't have you tripping over each other's feet."

"Do you want me to pick him up when he goes home tonight?"

"No need. We know where he lives. We know where he works. We can find him at any time."

"You don't want me to try to take him out?"

"No, this man has proven himself much too dangerous. I'm bringing in an asset. The man is an expert. You'll meet him and point out the target. He'll do the rest."

"Yes, sir. Do you want me to do whatever he says?"

"He won't say anything."

29.

AZIZ STOOD IMPASSIVE, waiting for the assignment.

"You're going to Paris. You'll leave at once." Fahd texted him a photo of Barnett that he'd received from Glenville. "This is the target. At least, this is how he looks now. Two days ago he looked entirely different. He may look different tomorrow. It doesn't matter. Glenville will point him out."

Without moving a muscle, Aziz managed to convey what he felt about Glenville.

"The target is at the embassy to ferret out our agent. This must not happen. This must be handled quickly and without fuss. We do not need the French police on high alert. Not now. Not when we are all set. This operation must come off without a hitch."

Aziz didn't have to nod agreement. He was always in agreement.

"This man is a problem," Fahd said. "I have no time for problems. When we arrive in Paris next week, he must be gone."

30.

THE AGENT AT the front desk was confused. "You wish to see Special Agent Norton?"

"That's right," Teddy said.

"But you don't have an appointment?"

"No, I do not."

"Special Agent Norton is the station chief."

"I know."

"What is it you wish to see him about?"

"CIA business."

"Yes, of course. What specifically do you mean?"

"I have business with Agent Norton. I can't tell you what it is because it's classified. But it's high priority, and I need to see him at once."

"You understand the problem?"

"Yes, I do. *You* are the problem. You only deal with matters that are routine. Anything important is above your pay grade."

The agent flushed. "Now, see here."

"You have my credentials. Run them."

"Sir?"

"Run my credentials. Shouldn't you know who you're dealing with before you refuse to let me in?"

The agent gave him a look, then turned to the computer. He punched in the code on the credentials. Immediately, a file came up.

The agent blinked. "This is *all* classified."

Teddy nodded. "Most of it. There's probably some stuff that isn't, but it won't be very interesting."

"What's your point?"

Teddy groaned. Back in his years at the bureau, this young man wouldn't have lasted a day. "Now you know what to tell your station chief. An agent, with such highly classified status you can't access it, wants to see him. What would he like you to do?"

Minutes later a rather wary Station Chief Norton ushered Teddy into his office.

"I'm Special Agent Norton, Paris station chief."

"Pleased to meet you. Agent Felix Dressler."

"What can I do for you, Agent Dressler?"

"To begin with, you could teach the young man at the front desk his job. An agent shouldn't have to jump through hoops to see you."

"To be fair, he didn't know who you were."

"Neither do you, but you let me in."

"I'm in charge of this station. I can do whatever I want without being second-guessed."

"To a certain extent that's true."

Agent Norton bristled. "Are you trying to tell me something?"

"Absolutely not. For the moment, we're just sparring with words."

"Why are you here?"

"I was brought out of deep cover and assigned to report to this station."

"Why?"

"That's a good question. I'm sure there's a reason. There's usually a reason for what the powers that be do."

"You don't know why you're here?"

"I didn't say that. As to a specific assignment, it's sort of open-ended, but I was told I'd receive your full cooperation."

Norton wasn't happy with the answer. Teddy hadn't expected him to be.

"Are we being reassessed?"

"Certainly not."

"What would you tell me if we *were* being reassessed?"

"That you're not being reassessed."

Norton bit his lip.

Teddy smiled. "Hey, I'm on your side. Let's work together."

"What did you have in mind?"

"I'd like to meet your field agents."

"I thought you might."

"Will that be a problem?"

"Some of them are in the field."

"I'd like to meet the ones that aren't."

"Of course." Norton picked up the phone. "Felson. Send in Morrow, Reynolds, and Rowan." He put down the phone and said, ironically, "Anything else you'd like?"

"Could I get a printout of the personnel?"

"Sure. Just fill out a requisition form."

Teddy smiled slightly. "So, you're not concerned about being reassigned?"

Norton tried to stare him down, but Teddy didn't blink. "But you're *not* reassessing the station," Norton said sarcastically.

"Absolutely not," Teddy said.

After a moment, Norton gave in and picked up the phone again.

31.

Agent Morrow was pudgy, as if he'd gone soft on the job from a combination of French food and not too much action. Teddy wasn't sure if that made him more suspicious or less.

Agent Reynolds was wiry and athletic-looking. He seemed cocky, almost insolent. Teddy couldn't tell if that was a defense mechanism or just who he was.

Agent Rowan was younger and more attractive. Or perhaps she just *seemed* younger because she was more attractive. At any rate, Teddy was impressed. Agent Rowan would not at all be unpleasant to investigate.

The other two agents seemed to be vying to appear macho in front of her.

"I don't get it," Agent Reynolds said. "You're sent here for an undisclosed reason, and we're supposed to just take you in?"

"Yeah, I probably wouldn't like me much, either," Teddy said.

"So where are you from?" Agent Morrow asked.

"You name it, I've been there."

"I meant just now."

"I know you did," Teddy said.

Morrow flushed slightly.

"He's been sent to work with us," Norton said. "For an undisclosed purpose even *he* may not know."

"Bullshit," Agent Reynolds said.

"My sentiments exactly," Teddy said. "Frankly, I wasn't happy to get the assignment. But don't hold it against me, I don't like most of what I do. May I assume since you're all here you're not specifically assigned?"

"Were you hoping to assign them?" Agent Norton said.

"I'm hoping to learn soon what the CIA wants of me and get out of your hair," Teddy said. "In the meantime, if something comes up, I'm here. Not that I'm expecting anything. I'm trying to figure out if you are."

Agent Rowan smiled. She had a nice smile. "That's so reasonable it's hard to hate you."

"Trust me, people always find a way." Teddy referred to the printout he'd been given. "Okay, that's Morrow, Reynolds, and Rowan. So I assume Agents Paul and Workman are on assignment?"

Agent Reynolds looked at Norton accusingly. "How come *he* has a roster?"

"He asked," Norton said. "You want one, I'll make you a copy."

FOR THE REST of the day, Teddy went through the tedious process of investigating the lower-level office personnel. Any one of them could have been the mole, but Teddy tended to doubt it. The person he was looking for would have more access to sensitive material than the average desk jockey. Still, he put secretaries through their paces and got a feel for the bookkeeper's grasp on the workings of the organization.

Agent Reynolds went with him. Teddy said there was no need, he had the printout, and he could find the people by himself, but Agent Reynolds wasn't buying it. Under the guise of camaraderie, a thin ruse that fooled no one, he insisted on showing Teddy around. It didn't matter. As far as Teddy could see, everything was open and aboveboard. Routine matters were being handled, and none of the people who were handling them were showing any of the nervousness someone with something to hide would.

The first agent of any interest was a young man named Jacques who sat scrolling through screens on his computer. It was near the end of the tour, and Agent Reynolds was taking a bathroom break.

Jacques smiled when Teddy introduced himself. "You're new? I wouldn't know. People don't stop by my desk that often. They think I'm a computer nerd."

"Whatever gives them that idea?"

Jacques frowned, then his face lit up in a big smile. He pointed to his computer. "Yes, yes, good one. That's what I am."

"What do you do at the computer?"

"I monitor reservations."

"You mean plane reservations?"

"Yes. And hotel. Not so glamorous, but every now and then something comes up. Like the arms conference a few years back."

" 'Arms conference'?"

"Well, not an official conference, of course, but a bunch of international arms dealers met in Paris to buy and sell. They haven't tried that again. It didn't go very well for them."

"Nothing since?" Teddy said.

"Nothing that ever pans out. I got a hit last week, of a suspected arms dealer coming to town. A couple of them, actually, both staying at l'Arrington Hotel. It looked promising, perhaps a clandestine business meeting, but it turned out they were both there for other purposes entirely."

"That's disappointing."

"Not at all. I'd rather have nothing going on than get a pat on the back for finding something."

"Are you French?"

Jacques smiled his big smile again. "What gave me away?"

"Then you would know. Where's a good place to get a cup of coffee around here in the morning?"

"Ah. Café du Soleil. Right around the corner. Ask anyone."

Teddy thanked him and moved on to the next desk.

Agent Reynolds came back from the bathroom. Before joining Teddy, he stopped to talk to Jacques.

"What was he asking you about?"

Jacques looked after Teddy, then back at the agent. "A place to eat."

32.

Teddy finished his interviews without incident. He'd been there two hours and hadn't seen anything particularly suspicious. Lance would think he was slipping.

Teddy left the embassy and strolled a few blocks, looking at the novelties in shop windows. As expected, Agent Reynolds was following him. Luckily, his shadow was not. It would have been hard to lose one and not the other.

Teddy walked one more block just to make sure Agent Reynolds was the only one taking an interest in him, and hailed a cab. He took it straight to the Gare de Lyon railway station, got out, and went downstairs to the bank of long-term lockers. He opened locker 26, which contained ten thousand dollars and Melvin Melbourne's passport. He took out five hundred dollars, closed the locker, and left, making sure Agent Reynolds was close enough to have seen what he did.

Outside, he took evasive action, just good enough to be convincing, but not good enough to be effective. After that, he led Agent Reynolds to his apartment. He went in, sat on the bed, and looked around. It was every bit as depressing as a deep-cover agent's apartment should be.

Teddy took out a burner phone and called Dino. "Everything all set?"

"Hey, it's not rocket science," Dino said.

"That's why I ask. You're a police commissioner. You can command a citywide task force. It doesn't mean you can tie your shoe."

"Viv usually helps me with that. This was not a problem."

"You're there now?"

"Yes."

"Where is it?"

Dino relayed the address. Teddy didn't write it down. He didn't need to, and he didn't want to create a document he had to worry about people seeing.

Teddy left the apartment. He went through the same elusive measures as before, only subtly more effective. Within minutes, Agent Reynolds was nowhere to be seen. Teddy figured the young man would use the opportunity to search his apartment and check out the railway locker.

It was a ten-minute taxi ride, far enough for comfort, but not so far as to be annoying. Teddy got out two blocks away. He walked down the street to a small town house. He went up on the stoop and rang the bell for 2A. Moments later he was buzzed in the door.

He went upstairs and found Dino waiting with the apartment door open.

"It's about time," Dino said. "This is a depressing place to have to hang out in."

"Well, that's encouraging," Teddy said. "I see you know my taste in dwellings."

The apartment was indeed drab, not unlike the other one Teddy had rented. A suitcase stood just inside the door.

"You didn't unpack for me?" Teddy said.

"I didn't want a lecture on snooping through your things."

"Well, this is exactly what I need. An apartment no one knows about to balance out the apartment everyone knows about."

"Except you have to make sure you're not followed every time you use it."

"So?"

"Isn't that a major pain in the ass?"

"You loved making sure you weren't followed, and you know it."

"I was supposed to make sure I wasn't followed?"

Teddy's cell phone rang—that is, his Dressler cell phone. He took it out. "Hello?"

"Felix?"

It took him a second to realize that was him. "Yes?"

"This is Kristin Rowan. I'm one of the many agents you met today."

"Actually, I remember you. Probably because you weren't a snotty hard-ass."

She laughed. "I looked for you and you'd left."

"I make my own hours. It's one of the perks of the job."

"I tried that once. Norton docked me."

"How'd you get my number?"

"I'm a CIA agent."

"They teach you things like that?"

"Yeah, codes and stuff. You want me to show you?"

"Is that why you called?"

"I was actually wondering what you were doing for dinner."

"I'm new in town. I have no plans."

"You do now. Meet me at six in front of the Sacré-Coeur."

"Where is that?"

"I thought you were an agent," she said, and hung up.

33.

AGENT KRISTIN ROWAN had taken time to change from her office clothes into a simple, red sheath dress. Teddy appreciated the effort, and the result. She glided up to him on the steps of the Sacré-Coeur and completely upstaged the imposing stone basilica.

She smiled. "Well, I see you found it."

"Was that deliberate?"

"What?"

"Choosing the Sacré-Coeur. I had to ask my cabbie where one of the most famous landmarks in Paris was. Now, the Louvre I'd have known, or the Arc de Triomphe. But the Sacré-Coeur I wasn't sure."

"Did that make you feel foolish?"

"I always feel foolish around attractive women. I don't have to look for an excuse. In our business, embarrassment is a luxury. Shall we have dinner?"

"I hope so. I made reservations."

"Where?"

"Where do you think?"

"I couldn't possibly guess. There're a number of popular, trendy restaurants, but you would never go there.

You eat where the locals eat. You picked some little place no one's heard of, but everyone has a cousin who's tipped them off about."

"My hairdresser, actually."

"I can't wait."

KRISTIN'S RESTAURANT WAS everything Teddy had predicted it would be, a hole-in-the-wall on the first floor of what appeared to be a private home. It was so non-commercial, it had no name. At least none was proclaimed on the menu. On Kristin's advice, they simply ordered the daily special. They sipped wine, nibbled bread, and smiled at each other.

"I don't know what I'm allowed to ask you," Kristin said.

"Such as?"

"You just got here. Are you settled in?"

"I have an apartment. Agent Reynolds is probably searching it now."

"Do you know that?"

"No, but that's what I'd do. The problem with this job is that it breeds paranoia. At least that's been my experience. You don't look like you're afraid of anything."

"You really know how to flatter a girl, don't you? It's not 'How gorgeous you are,' it's 'Gee, you're tough as nails.'"

"Tell me about yourself."

"Haven't you read my file?"

"Have you read mine?"

"How? It's redacted. You were never on a mission that wasn't classified. I suppose this one will be, too."

"More than likely."

"How can you say that? You don't even know what it is yet."

"I know it's top secret."

"How do you know that?"

"Because I'm on it."

"Oh, big-time spy. Is that how you get the girls?"

"You're confusing me with James Bond."

"Don't knock James Bond. He's the reason I joined the Agency. I wanted to *be* James Bond. I wanted to do the things he does."

"Oh, really?"

"Well, not seduce girls, but the rest of it. I wanted to shoot bad guys and win at chemin de fer, and sit eye to eye with megalomaniacs who wanted to rule the world, and escape from their armed fortresses. It seemed so glamorous."

"And was it?"

"I got posted in Pittsburgh and Paris. No maniacs have tried to rule them yet. Of course, you know this from my file."

"I know what it *says*. I didn't know your attitude about it. Are you married?"

"Divorced. My husband was an insurance salesman. Couldn't get used to living with a spy. In retrospect, I can't blame him. I treated him like a civilian. What about you?"

"I was married. My wife's dead. A car accident a couple of years ago. I'm still not over it."

She looked in his eyes. "With you I can't tell what's true and what's deep cover."

"Does it matter?"

"Did *she* know you were a spy?"

"Why? Didn't your husband?"

She smiled. "You're very good at what you do."

"I don't even know what that is."

"Neither do I, but you're very good at it. Has there been anyone since?"

"There was a woman for a while, but we live in different places. How about you?"

"Not really. That damn fool agent thinks he's in love with me. As if he had any chance."

"Reynolds?"

"No, not him. Morrow. Believe me, I've done nothing to encourage him."

"I believe you. After all, you've done nothing to encourage me."

"Except ask you out to dinner. Why do you think I did that?"

"I think you're highly competitive. I think every agent at the station wants to find out why I'm here, and you want to be first."

"You don't think it's your devilish charm?"

"I was being modest."

She smiled. "So what's it going to take to find out what you're doing here?"

"You could ask me."

"What are you doing here?"

"I came to Paris to pick up attractive spies."

"How's that going for you?"

"I'll tell you tomorrow."

34.

WHEN TEDDY WOKE up she was gone. He sat up in bed and looked around her apartment. He hadn't paid much attention to it the night before. It was only slightly cheerier than his. She'd had time to decorate it, but there was little evidence of a woman's touch.

Teddy's jacket was lying over a chair. It was in a slightly different position than when he'd left it. Teddy smiled. She'd gone through his clothes. He'd have been disappointed if she hadn't.

She had left a note. *You don't have hours, but I do. See you there. Act casual.*

Teddy grinned. He found he was getting quite a kick out of Kristin.

Teddy got dressed and headed out. He used evasive action, but no one was watching the apartment. He hailed a cab, got out a block from the embassy, and asked a passerby for the Café du Soleil. It was a little coffee shop down a sunny side street. There were tables out front, but Jacques wasn't there. Teddy peeked in the door and found him sitting over a cup of coffee. His laptop was open on the table in front of him.

"So that's why you like this café. They have Internet."

Jacques looked up and smiled. "Ah, you took my suggestion."

"You seem like a man whose opinion I can count on."

"Please, sit down."

"Thank you."

Teddy sat and ordered an espresso and a croissant.

"I checked you out," Jacques said.

"Oh? Why?"

"Because everyone else did. Right after you left, Agent Reynolds wanted to know what you were asking about."

"What did you tell him?"

"I told him you were looking for a place to eat."

"Was he happy to hear it?"

"He didn't seem happy."

"I get the impression he really isn't. I'm glad you didn't tell him about l'Arrington."

"Why?"

"Because I don't know what it means yet, and until I do, people underfoot are a nuisance."

"Do you think there's something to it?"

"*You* did."

"What makes you say that?"

"You told me about it."

"Yes, I did."

"Why?"

"I suppose I was passing the buck."

"Your English idiom is very good."

Jacques frowned. "You don't want to know what I mean?"

"I know exactly what you mean. You think the reservations at l'Arrington mean something. But you've made your report, no one took it seriously, and you don't want to become known as a pest. On the other hand, if I take an interest, you're off the hook."

Jacques grinned. "Got me. Am I no longer your friend?"

"No, I like you even better. All right, here's the deal. I'd like to know a little more about these reservations. Check them out again, see if anything else pops up. Though let's not bring it up at the Agency. This is just between you and me. Are you here the same time every morning?"

"More or less."

"Let's make it more. See if there are any more bookings of that nature, and get me some details on the ones you found. We'll meet back here tomorrow. Is that all right with you?"

"It is." Jacques put up his hands apologetically. "I would kind of like to know who I'm dealing with."

Teddy smiled. "You accessed my files and got nothing."

"Yes."

"May I use your laptop?"

"You can't access Agency files from here."

"Let me see." Teddy swung the computer around, typed in a few codes, and swung it back. Felix Dressler's file was on the screen.

Jacques was astonished. "How did you do that?"

"Want to see another trick? I'll open one of the classified missions for you."

Teddy opened a file labeled Afghanistan, K&R.

"That's *kidnap and ransom*. It was a clandestine mission because the United States doesn't ransom prisoners."

"But you do?"

"Not at all. But the enemy thought I would, and we got our prisoner back. Now then. That's who I am, and that's the type of thing I do. Read about it, and close the file. Don't worry about security. When you close it, it won't open again.

"Anyway, that's a glimpse at who I am. You have to make up your mind about me. I'm gambling that you'll do the right thing. I'll be here tomorrow morning. I hope you will, too."

"That's all you want to know? About the reservations at l'Arrington?"

"For starters. When I hear what you've found, I hope it leads to something else."

Jacques took a breath. "I'll be here."

"Good."

Teddy stood up and tossed money on the table. "I'll leave first," he said.

He figured Jacques would like that.

35.

TEDDY WALKED A few blocks until he found a hotel. He went in as if he belonged there and asked if they had computers for the guests. The concierge directed him to the back of the lobby where a small business office was set up with computers, a printer, and even a fax machine. Teddy logged on to one of the computers and sent an encrypted e-mail to Millie Martindale reporting his progress. It was short, as there was none. He logged off, and left the hotel.

Teddy went back to the apartment Dino had rented for him, the one no one knew about. Nonetheless, he checked to see that it was undisturbed, and that no one had planted any bugs. When he was satisfied, he took out a new burner phone and called Kevin Cushman in Washington, D.C.

Kevin was not a part of the federal government, at least not officially, but Teddy had used him on occasion. Kevin lived with his mother and spent most of the day lounging around in his pajamas playing video games. That, coupled with his screen name, Warplord924, gave the impression he was a college dropout, but Kevin was actually a well-respected computer technician pulling down six figures a year.

Kevin was glad to hear from him. "Is this who I think it is?"

"It is. And thank you for not saying the name."

"I'm not sure I know the name."

"I'm grateful nonetheless."

"Is this an official call?"

"It is."

"What do you need?"

"Something impossible."

"I'm your man."

"I need to know if there's been an Internet search for a particular name. Can it be done?"

"It depends on how it's trending. How many searches are we talking about?"

"One."

"You want to know if *one* person has searched for this name?"

"I know it doesn't sound promising."

"Hey, you had me at 'impossible.'"

"Can it be done?"

"It'll be tough. You take any given name and *someone* will have searched for it *sometime*."

"Within the last two days."

"That helps. Tell me, you didn't do an Internet search for this guy yourself, did you? Because then I'd get a false positive."

"I didn't. Can you do it?"

"Hang on, I'm thinking."

"I'll mark it on my calendar."

"Huh?"

"That's the first time I gave you something hard enough you had to think about it."

"This is going to take a little time. Can I call you back?"

"All right, just this once. But after that, I contact you."

"Gotcha. What's the name you're tracing?"

"This time it's Melvin Melbourne."

"'This time'? Boy, you give a guy an inch," Kevin said, and hung up.

HE CALLED BACK fifteen minutes later. "No one has searched for Melvin Melbourne in the last two days."

"Can you tell me how you know?"

"How much time have you got?"

"Point taken. So you can search for any name but I can't?"

"Unless you want to start computer classes."

"Okay. Keep checking on that name. If you get a hit, can you tell if the search originated in Paris?"

"Of course."

"In that case, make a note and we'll discuss it the next time we talk. It's probably just my quarry satisfying his curiosity. But if you get a search originating in another country, that's pay dirt. In that case, send me an encrypted e-mail with the word *yes*. If I need to, I'll get in touch."

"Will do. Is that all?"

"Until I give you the next name."

TEDDY WENT BACK to the embassy and asked the young man at the front desk for Agent Norton. This time he was shown right in.

"So," Norton said, "any progress?"

"Nothing worth reporting. I just wanted to give you a heads-up."

"Oh?"

"From what I've observed, there's nothing much going on at the moment. I'm probably the most exciting thing that's happened in months. Your agents are eager to know what I'm about. It occurs to me I may be followed, and since your men are good, I wouldn't necessarily know it. While I'm in Paris—while I'm in any city, for that matter—I keep getaway money and a spare passport in a locker at the train station. Should one of your agents report this, just keep it quiet, will you? Don't put it in a report or pass it on to the other agents. It's just between you and me."

"You're planning on taking off?"

"I'd hate to break your heart, but if I'm given a pressing assignment, yes."

"Will they tell you what it is?"

Teddy smiled.

"Two other field agents are here today, if you'd like to meet them."

"I hope they didn't come in from the cold just to meet me," Teddy said. Norton ignored the comment, but Teddy got the impression that Paris was not typically an active enough location to merit undercover work. "So who have we got?"

"Agent Valerie Paul was particularly eager to meet you."

"By all means. Show her in."

Valerie Paul was the type of woman who might have been the Paris office's sexy shill, if they hadn't happened to already have Kristin Rowan. Teddy wondered if that rankled. Valerie had brown hair, blue eyes, and a suspicious nature. Teddy knew she'd be following him from the moment he said hello.

"So what are you doing here, Agent Dressler?" she asked.

"I'm here on assignment, so something is going to happen. I've been talking to the people at the Agency trying to figure out what that is."

She smiled. "And you expect me to believe that?"

"I'd be disappointed if you did. I doubt if they sent me here just to find out if agents were gullible." Before she could respond, he added, "So what are *you* doing here? I understand you're on assignment."

"Just routine. There are certain foreign nationals we keep track of when they're in town. I handed off my assignment to Agent Kristin Rowan early this morning. I believe you met her yesterday."

"I probably did," Teddy said. "I met so many agents."

Valerie smiled. "Yes. She said I'd find you deflective."

"That was actually in my profile, before I got it redacted."

The intercom buzzed. Norton picked it up, listened, and said, "Send him in."

A young agent came in. He was slightly shorter than Agent Reynolds, but a rough-and-ready type. Teddy would have picked him in a fight. He looked like he needed a shave. It went with his image.

"This is Agent Workman," Norton said. "Agent Workman, this is Agent Dressler, temporarily on assignment."

Workman shook Teddy's hand. "'Temporarily'?"

Teddy shrugged. "I go where they tell me."

"And they told you to come here?"

"Yes."

"What for?"

"I assume they're preparing for something."

"They haven't told you what?"

"They never tell me more than they have to. You know how it goes."

Agent Workman gave a look as if he didn't really know how it goes at all. As if, in fact, he felt Teddy was full of bullshit. Teddy couldn't blame him.

"Look, guys, I'm on your side. I won't be able to prove it until something happens, but when it does, you'll be glad to have me. In the meantime, what do you say we get out of the station chief's hair, and let me treat you to a cup of coffee."

"Coffee's free."

"Even better."

Teddy took them down to the commissary. Jacques looked up from his computer as they went by, but it was just a casual glance. He didn't try to catch Teddy's eye.

They got themselves coffee and sat at one of the tables.

"All right," Teddy said. "Now that we're not being judged by the boss, let's get down to brass tacks. Something happened here, and someone knows what it is. I don't necessarily mean in the Agency, it could be something in town. Whatever it was, it was enough to raise a red flag and result in my presence. So what's been going on recently? Is there any little thing—any incident—that could have raised the alarm?"

"Rami disappeared," Workman said. Valerie shot him a glance. "Well, he asked. It's not like we fucked up or anything. It's something that happened in the last few weeks."

"Tell me about it."

"Not much to tell. We monitor certain foreign diplomats."

"If you can call them diplomats," Valerie said.

"That is the polite term. *Enemy agents* or *spies* would be more accurate. Anyway, one of the Middle Eastern agents we were concerned with—Rami, a Syrian—was here for a few days and we were keeping tabs. Suddenly he was gone. It doesn't have to mean anything. People change their plans. People get called home."

"Was this of any particular concern?"

"None. It's the sort of thing that happens from time to time. But when you ask for any incident, we're hard-pressed to come up with one. That's the only one I can think of, and that's stretching it."

"I'll say," Valerie said. She seemed more than a little defensive. Teddy wondered if she had been on duty when the man disappeared.

"Was there anything to indicate the man had dropped out of sight, as opposed to just going home?"

"It was sudden and unexpected," Workman said.

"Why? What did you expect him to do?"

"We expected him to be in town for a week. That's what his plans were. He'd only been here two days when he dropped off the map."

"Could it be because he noticed he was under surveillance?"

Valerie bristled. "No, but if you want to take it that way, feel free."

"It's a tough business," Teddy said. "You're watching people, someone else is watching you. Somehow or other it all means something, but you can't spend your time wondering if you had a good day. I'm just trying to sort out what happened. I'm trying to figure out why, and what you base your opinion on. If you were under the impression that you were spotted, that would support your conclusion that the guy took off. But no one's blaming you. Don't fall into Norton's trap. He thinks I'm here to reassess the station. He's afraid for his job. Don't be afraid for yours."

"That isn't what I'm thinking at all," Valerie Paul said.

"I'm glad to hear it. This guy who disappeared—Rami—how'd you know he planned to be here for a week?"

"That's how long his hotel reservation was."

"He was staying at a hotel? Which one?"

"L'Arrington."

36.

TEDDY LED Valerie Paul to the Gare de Lyon railway station. He opened locker 27, which had Daniel Remington's passport, and took out five hundred dollars. Then he led her back to his apartment. Having spent the previous night at Kristin's, Teddy hadn't been back since he had led Agent Reynolds there.

Teddy checked the apartment out. The lock on the door had been picked. It was skillfully done. Still, Teddy could see fresh scratches. He went in and searched the apartment for bugs. He found one in the radiator grille and one in the overhead lamp. Those were easy to find, so Teddy suspected a third. He found it inside the roller of the window blind. Teddy destroyed the first two, but left the third one in place. It was important to let the agents think they were winning.

Agent Valerie Paul was lurking down the street when Teddy left. He ditched her, so she'd have a chance to check out the train station, and he'd have a chance to see his friends.

———

STONE'S MEWS HOUSE was on a quiet, cobblestone lane. The gate still had the massive wooden doors and sentry posts from when it had been a safe house. After the CIA had had occasion to house him there, Stone liked it so much he bought it. With his typical self-assurance, he'd had the living room refurnished, including carpeting, artwork, and a grand piano, before even making an offer to Lance.

The house had four bedrooms—including the master, which took up an entire floor. It had a small servants' quarters and a garage that came equipped with a Mercedes.

Considering Stone didn't spend that much time in Paris, and also had access to the Royal Suite at l'Arrington, the little mews house was quite sufficient for his needs.

Stone and Dino were enjoying a fine cabernet in front of the fire when Teddy came in.

"Wine?" Teddy said.

"We're in France," Stone said. "I have to make concessions."

"Come, warm your feet by the fire," Dino said.

"My feet are perfectly warm."

"The thrill is that you can. It's a decadent luxury you don't normally get. Do you have a working fireplace in L.A.?"

"Yes."

"Spoilsport."

"So, did you crack the case yet?" Stone said.

"No. I met five field agents, any of whom could be the mole."

"Well, don't find him too soon," Dino said. "Tonight we're going to the Folies Bergère."

"Care to join us?" Stone said.

"I'm chasing down a lead."

"Oh. Does it look promising?"

"She looks very promising. I don't think she's the mole, but she's a wonderful lead." Teddy changed the subject. "So, where's my equipment?"

"It's locked up."

"Can I see?"

"Sure."

Stone got up and led the way into the study. A massive floor safe stood in the corner. Stone spun the dial and swung the door open. Teddy's equipment bag was on its own shelf.

"Perfect," Teddy said. "I don't feel confident leaving it unsecured." His cell phone rang, and he dug it out of his pocket.

It was Kristin. "I'm running late. Can you meet me for dinner?"

"Of course. Where?"

"Eight-thirty at Le Meurice."

"Le Meurice?" Teddy looked inquiringly at Stone.

Stone nodded. "Expensive."

"Isn't that a little pricey for a girl on an Agency salary?"

"It's all right, you're paying," Kristin said, and hung up.

37.

TEDDY SMILED AT Kristin over the rim of his cappuccino. They had just finished a leisurely and delicious dinner in the opulent eighteenth-century dining room, and he was feeling good.

"You haven't asked me about my assignment."

"I figure if there'd been any progress you'd have told me."

"Smart girl."

"I, on the other hand, had a very eventful day."

"Doing what?"

"Following the undersecretary of Germany around so that Agent Valerie Paul could meet you."

"Nice of you."

"Nice had nothing to do with it. Valerie wouldn't take no for an answer."

"She struck me as sane and sensible in a castrating sort of way."

Kristin smiled. "Did she make any catty references about me?"

"No, but I wasn't having dinner with her. I was just trying to explain that I wasn't after her job."

"Her job?"

"There is a feeling in the Agency, probably filtered down from Norton, that I'm here solely to assess the Paris station and see if changes need to be made."

"Are you?"

"No, but if I were, I'd deny it, so it was tough to reassure her. I wouldn't be surprised if she was spying on us from one of the other tables."

"Not on a CIA salary."

"Indeed. What made you think I could afford this place?"

"Anyone under such deep cover would require immediate access to money. Your entire file is redacted. You do the math."

Teddy pointed at the check, which had been discreetly slipped onto the table, along with the coffee and cognac. "I've been wondering how I'm going to justify a thousand-dollar dinner on the expense account."

"This dinner was crucial to your operation."

"Oh?"

"I have valuable information. You were hoping to get me inebriated to loosen my tongue."

"Yes, I was, but it had nothing to do with getting information."

They finished up their coffee, and Teddy settled the bill.

On their way out, Kristin said, "I'm going to the ladies. I'll meet you outside."

Teddy walked out the front door. With his peripheral vision, he could see his shadow watching from the street corner.

———

A LITTLE MAN built like a fireplug stepped from the shadows and aimed a gun at the back of Teddy's head.

Teddy whirled and chopped down on his arm. The gun flew from the little man's hand and skittered across the street.

Teddy didn't go for his own gun. He wanted the little man alive.

The little man bent over. Teddy aimed a kick at the back of his head.

It was Teddy's turn to be surprised. With amazing agility for one so short and stocky, the little man ducked the kick, grabbed Teddy's leg, flipped him sideways, and plowed in.

Teddy hit the ground rolling. He struggled to his knees and managed to block the blows aimed at his head.

"Felix!"

Teddy glanced up.

Kristin stood under a streetlight. Her hand flew to her purse and came out with a gun.

The little man saw her. He scowled, turned, and fled.

Kristin stood watching him go.

Teddy got to his feet.

"Who the hell was that?" Kristin said.

"I don't know, but he seemed to resent my presence."

"This isn't funny," Kristin said. "Someone just tried to kill you. Isn't it time you stop playing games and tell us why?"

"I don't know why. I've never seen that man in my life.

I hope I never see him again. I'm very glad you scared him off." Teddy glanced around. "Where's his gun?"

"What gun?"

"He had a gun. I knocked it away."

"I didn't see a gun. I must have come along just after."

"It skidded across the street." Teddy pointed. "It should be over there."

"It's not."

"The other guy must have got it."

"What other guy?"

Teddy waved it away. "A routine shadow. He's not important."

Kristin was incredulous. "'Not important'? Why the hell was someone stalking you outside the restaurant?"

"Maybe he figured anyone who could afford to eat there would have to have money."

"Come on, Felix. Why are you so important?"

Teddy sighed. "I wish I knew."

38.

GLENVILLE CAUGHT UP with Aziz two blocks away. He'd been calling his name, but Aziz paid no attention. Finally Glenville grabbed him by the arm.

Aziz spun with every intention of delivering a fatal blow.

"Can't you hear me?" Glenville said, suddenly realizing he might not be able to. The man was mute. Some mutes were also deaf. He extended the weapon. "Your gun. I managed to pick it up."

Aziz took the gun. If he appreciated the effort, he didn't show it.

Glenville sighed. This was not his day. And the surly hit man was the least of it. Reluctantly, he pulled his cell phone out of his pocket.

Fahd had been waiting for the call. "Is it done?"

"No. The man is good. Aziz surprised him, but he disarmed Aziz and they fought hand to hand."

"Aziz didn't win?"

"No. Another agent surprised him and he took off."

"Another agent?"

"Yes. A woman. She had a gun."

Fahd rolled his eyes. "Oh, for God's sake! Did Aziz leave his gun behind?"

"No, I managed to retrieve it. We can try again tomorrow."

"Just tell me when it's done. Is Aziz there?"

"Yes."

"Put him on the phone."

Aziz took the phone and put it to his ear.

"Are you there?" Fahd said.

Aziz snapped the phone with his finger.

"Good," Fahd said. "Glenville doesn't need to know this, but you do. We need to get the job done, and we need to get it done before we arrive in Paris next week. I want this man taken care of at all costs. Kill him if you can, but if you can't, I want him gone. Do you understand me? I don't care if we have to sacrifice our mole. I want him out of town. He won't leave until he finds the mole. So if you can't kill him, kill the mole."

39.

AGENT WORKMAN WAS outside Kristin's building when Teddy emerged the next morning. Teddy wondered if it was proprietary, if the young agent had designs on Kristin. It was not unlikely, and it would complicate things somewhat, and make his motives more difficult to sort out.

Kristin was still sleeping. Teddy wondered if Workman would follow him, or stay behind to confront her. He walked down the street a block. Workman was following him. Teddy wondered if it was too early for the train station. He thought not. He hailed a cab, and took it to the Gare de Lyon railway station. He went inside and opened the box of Arnold Mycroft.

Teddy went outside prepared to ditch the young agent, but he didn't have to. Workman stayed behind, presumably to search the locker.

Teddy hailed a cab and took it to the Café du Soleil.

Jacques was at his table. He looked pleased with himself. He could barely contain himself while Teddy ordered coffee.

"I have all the details," Jacques said. "I don't know what to make of them, but I found the connection."

"What do you mean?"

"It turns out the men I flagged are all registered for a conference at l'Arrington next week. It's a science conference and exhibition with over fourteen hundred attendees."

"A science conference? What are they exhibiting?"

"Rare animals."

Teddy blinked. "What?"

"That's right. In addition to presentations and lectures, there will be select exhibits of rare animals and insects. Top zoologists from around the world will be attending."

"As well as foreign arms dealers?"

"Yes, but not many. They're what tipped me off to the convention, but their presence is not at all significant."

"How can that be?"

"Well, in the Syrian party, for instance, we have Fahd Kassin—a Syrian strongman, but not an arms dealer—his bodyguard, and three zoologists. Their interest would seem to be entirely in the animals. Fahd is likely accompanying the party to keep the scientists in check."

"What about the other arms dealers?"

"The same thing—all are part of a party that includes primarily zoologists."

Teddy frowned. "And what are people doing at this conference?"

"They have talks and panels and presentations scheduled, as well as a banquet."

"Which the Syrians are attending?"

"Yes. In fact, I hacked their website and downloaded their program. All the Syrians, and all the other men flagged, are attending one particular panel. It's a closed panel, by invitation only. 'Rarest of the Rare,' a lecture by a renowned biology professor."

"I see."

"There is one other common thread. Several of the conference attendees are also big-game hunters."

Teddy mouth dropped open. "And they're all attending that panel?"

"Yes, all of them."

"So there may be more to that panel than meets the eye. Keep digging. Let me know if you find something."

"How can I reach you?"

Teddy took out a spare burner phone and gave it to him. "Text me from this phone. No message, just an address. I'll meet you there."

"What address?"

"Choose someplace touristy, where there will be a lot of people. You don't have to say when. I'll come right away. Just text me where and go."

"You think it's that important?"

"*Something* has to be."

40.

TEDDY CHECKED IN at the Agency.

"You got something?" Norton said.

"I'm afraid not. I just wanted to alert you to an incident."

"Oh?"

"Agent Kristin Rowan and I were attacked last night after dinner."

"'Attacked'?"

"Mugged, really. I was the target. Two men set on me, and Agent Rowan came along and scared them away."

"Are you kidding me?"

"She was armed. She got the drop on them and they fled."

"Did you report this to the police?"

"No, we did not. I figured the Agency didn't need the gendarmes messing around in our business. They're not going to find anything, which means they'd be here forever searching for a motive."

"You're probably right. Where did this happen?"

"Outside Le Meurice."

"You dined at Le Meurice?"

"What can I say? I was trying to impress a young lady."

"Did it work?"

"It's hard to make an impression when you have to be rescued. *She* was impressive, though."

"You're treating this awfully cavalierly. Is there something about this attack you're not telling me?"

"One of the attackers had a gun. I knocked it away from him. Apparently the other one grabbed it because we couldn't find it."

"Did they demand money?"

"It never reached that stage. I reacted the moment I saw the gun. That led to a brief hand-to-hand skirmish before Agent Rowan broke it up."

"Were they trying to kill you?"

"Hard to say. A mugging certainly makes sense. I suppose the other agents should be on alert, but I think it's an isolated incident."

Norton frowned. He clearly wanted to say something, but couldn't think of what.

Teddy left the embassy. He was gratified to find Agent Morrow on his tail. Morrow was the only agent besides Kristin who hadn't tailed him yet. Teddy led him to the Gare de Lyon railway station. He went down and opened box 29, and took out a thousand dollars of Claude Fisher's money. He went back upstairs and managed to lose Agent Morrow in the station. The last thing

Teddy saw was the pudgy agent heading downstairs to search his locker.

His phone beeped with a text message.

It was from Jacques.

Top of Eiffel Tower.

41.

TEDDY GOT OUT of the elevator to find Jacques standing at the rail, looking out over the city. Teddy went up, leaned with his back against the rail, and cocked his head in Jacques's direction. "The Eiffel Tower?"

Jacques shrugged. "You said touristy."

"This better be good."

"It's not good, but it's something. I was mistaken when I said the Syrians had three zoologists in their party. Two of the professors are zoologists, but the third is a world-renowned microbiologist."

"Really?"

"Yes, and there are microbiologists in each party."

"Interesting."

"There's more. Some of the men flagged as weapons dealers are actually weapons designers and constructors. It was the word *weapons* that was flagged, not the word *dealers*."

"So this conference is actually about biological warfare?"

"As far as I can tell, the majority of the conference's presenters and attendees are legitimate. As is the programming, with the exception of that one particular panel they are all attending, along with their scientists. That is by invitation only, and could well be a front for something involving biological weapons."

Teddy thought that over. "Okay. Let's keep this between us for now. You say another subgroup of this panel is big-game hunters?"

"That's right. Though there is some overlap. Some of the big-game hunters are also into arms sales."

"Let's concentrate on them. Don't set off any alarms by investigating the microbiologists. Investigate the hunters. I'm particularly interested in any wealthy Americans who may be looking to spend big bucks to kill the rarest and most expensive big game. I want to know where they are, when they are going to get here, and where they intend to be in the meantime. Get me everything you can by tomorrow morning."

"Fine. Do I text you where to meet?"

Teddy smiled. "Sorry to spoil your fun, but I'll meet you at the café."

42.

As Teddy went down the Eiffel Tower, he checked to see if he was being followed. He wasn't. He took evasive maneuvers anyway, out of habit, then hopped in a cab and headed for Stone's house.

Stone met him at the door in his bathrobe.

"Just getting up?" Teddy said.

Stone led him into the living room and offered him a drink.

"Where's Dino?"

"He's having lunch with the prefect of police. I imagine they're talking shop."

"I hope he doesn't eat too much."

"Why is that?"

"I thought we might go out tonight, if you can arrange a dinner."

"I can always arrange a dinner. Luckily, I have nothing booked. What did you have in mind?"

A svelte Frenchwoman, wrapped in a towel and dripping wet—yet somehow still effortlessly elegant—padded into the room.

"Monsieur Stone, I am in the shower for twenty minutes. You said you would scrub my back."

"Yes, Monique, but you see we have a guest. Monique, Felix. Felix, Monique."

"Monsieur," she said to Teddy, "please do not think I do not like you, but you are keeping me from having a clean back."

Teddy grinned. "I did not realize you had a previous engagement, Stone. Don't worry, Monique, I won't be long."

Monique turned and padded out of the room.

"You were talking about dinner. What did you have in mind?"

"I was thinking of l'Arrington."

"Really? Coals to Newcastle in my case, but I'm happy to show it off."

"I was hoping your co-owner could join us."

"Marcel? I'm sure he'd love to, if there's nothing he can't get out of. Let me give him a call. Is there a particular reason you want to meet him?"

"I was hoping to get some information about the hotel."

Stone's eyebrows raised.

"I know you're the co-owner," Teddy said, "but he's always here and has more intimate knowledge of the day-to-day. I was hoping to get some information about the convention next week, but there's no reason to tell Marcel that. It may be nothing, and I don't want to alarm him."

"Now you're alarming me. What's happing at l'Arrington next week?"

"Animals."

43.

GLENVILLE PAID OFF the cab and hurried down the street after the three men who were his quarry. The taxi he'd been following had driven up to the front door of l'Arrington, and he'd been forced to stop half a block away. As he drew near, he saw the three men he knew to be Stone Barrington, Dino Bacchetti, and the one he was really concerned with, Billy Barnett—or whatever name he was using—go back into the very hotel where he'd picked them up to begin with. Slowing, so as not to overtake them, he smiled at the bellboys and the valet parkers for whom he offered no business, and pushed his way into the lobby.

Inside, a fuss was being made. Stone Barrington, recognized as the co-owner, was immediately descended upon by the concierge and the head clerk, eager to cater to his every whim. As if Stone were not enough of a celebrity himself, he was known to be dining with Marcel DuBois, which pushed his importance off the chart. The maître d' was summoned from the restaurant to personally escort them into the dining room.

Glenville watched all this with misgivings. Aziz would

want a quiet location to make another run at Barnett, some out-of-the-way place. At the owner's table in the main dining room—being catered to by waiters, wine stewards, and possibly the chef himself, would never do. Aziz would be displeased, and would probably find a way to blame him.

Glenville peeked into the dining room. Marcel Du-Bois was not there yet, but the other three men were being led to what was clearly his table. It commanded a view of the whole dining room, and was even slightly raised from the rest of the room.

Glenville sent Aziz a text: L'Arrington Hotel. Dining.

Aziz texted back: Check windows.

Glenville frowned. He didn't want to ask for a clarification, but "Check windows"?

Glenville went out and walked around to the side of the hotel where he figured the restaurant was. He had no problem finding it. The windows were all lit up in the gathering dark. While he watched, waiters scurried around the head table, pouring water and waiting to take drink orders. The maître d' was talking rapidly to the three men, no doubt apologizing for the absence of Monsieur DuBois, and imploring them to sit down. The men were demurring, probably not wanting to be seated before their host.

Through the brightly lit windows, Glenville could see it all in vivid detail. With a rush, he suddenly realized exactly what Aziz meant.

It was perfect.

44.

MARCEL WAS AN effusive, good-natured, congenial Frenchman. Of course, as co-owner of one of the finest hotels in Paris, he had reason to be happy. At the moment, however, he was unhappy to find himself in the hotel's private dining room.

"My friends, it is so good to see you. But we should be occupying a place of honor at my head table, where we can see and be seen and enjoy the atmosphere. The private dining room is perfect for lovers, but we are not lovers. We are men of the world. We should be dining in sight of the women of the world."

"That's my fault, Marcel," Teddy said. "There are people I do not want to see."

"They could be kept away from our table. Trust me, my men are good."

"It's a little more complicated than that. I had a couple of unfortunate incidents lately. It appears there are men who mean to do me harm."

"Have you gone to the police?"

"I don't want to involve the police."

"They can be discreet. Monsieur Bacchetti could intercede."

"I know he could, and I'm sure the French police could handle the situation. But, as I say, it's complicated. Protecting me won't serve any purpose."

"It will keep you alive."

"I suppose there's that," Teddy said.

"You joke in the face of death?"

"No, but I take precautions. This room is a precaution. I'm sorry to disappoint you, but it's perfect for my purpose."

Marcel put up his hands. "Please. I want to help if I can. What is the situation?"

"I'll tell you as much as I can without violating classified material, which I have not been given clearance to divulge. I'm here undercover, investigating a foreign threat. Some of the enemy have penetrated my cover and are trying to kill me. A sniper firing through a window into a brightly lit dining room would have an easy time of it. I apologize for requesting a private room."

Marcel considered that. "Under the circumstances, I have decided not to be offended."

AZIZ SHOWED UP carrying a rectangular metal case. It could have held a very expensive pool cue, but Glenville didn't think so. The hit man had brought his sniper rifle.

And Glenville had to disappoint him.

Glenville tapped out Changed rooms on his phone and held it up.

Aziz looked at him as if he were a moron, and tapped out on his own phone I can hear.

"Of course," Glenville said. "I'm sorry. They were taken to the head table, but they went to the private dining room, instead, away from any windows."

Aziz made no move, but Glenville could tell from his blank stare that the hit man was blaming him for the situation.

"You will have to wait for Barnett and his friends to come out. They are not staying at the hotel anymore, so they will be leaving when dinner is over."

In response, Aziz pointed to himself, then made a circular motion, gesturing at the building. Then he pointed at Glenville, and then to the ground. Without further ado, he turned his back on Glenville and walked around the side of the building, presumably to begin reconnaissance of the perimeter. Glenville sighed, assuming—but not entirely positive—that the mute assassin wanted him to stay here.

THE MEAL WAS spectacular, featuring chateaubriand sliced at the table, with a wide choice of sauces.

Teddy waited until the coffee and crème brûlée to casually bring up the subject. "You have a convention on rare animals next week?"

Marcel smiled. "Ah, you have seen the posters. Yes, this is a wonderful event, very popular. The entire hotel is booked for the whole week. You cannot get a room. The nearby hotels are also booked. People are staying many blocks away. Select smaller animals will be brought to the hotel for viewings. The larger animals will be stabled on a farm outside town, and guests will be bused there to see them."

"Is there a theme for the conference?"

"Oh, absolutely. Conservation. Many of these animals are endangered species. The hope is to attract money for programs working to prolong their existence. Besides showing the animals, the scientists will speak on panels and advocate for the vanishing breeds. Unfortunately, it isn't fair. Smaller animals can be shown during the talks. They have a chance to be adorable and win the heart. The larger animals can only be talked about and seen by those who choose to go by bus to the farm. I'm told this favors the smaller animals by better than two to one."

"Do you know anything about any specific panels?"

"Not much, but I could get you a brochure if you like. Let me send for one."

"I'll grab one on my way back to my apartment. Are all the panels open to everyone?"

"They are open to everyone registered for the convention. You could register for it. I think the fee is a few hundred euros."

"If I did that I could get into everything?"

Marcel frowned. "I want to say yes. I believe there are a couple of panels that are invitation only."

"Interesting," Teddy said. "Could you find out?"

"I can and I will," Marcel said. He took out his phone and punched in a number. "Alain. Marcel DuBois. I know it's after hours. If you will forgive me, I just had a quick question."

Apparently Alain was bending over backward to co-operate because it was not easy for Marcel to get a word in edgewise.

"Yes, yes, that's very nice of you. All I need to know is: I have a friend who is thinking of registering for the convention next week. He asked if his registration fee would get him into all the panels . . . Really? Which one is that? . . . I see. And how much would it take to get him into that one? . . . Invitation only? And how does one receive an invitation? . . . No, no, I would not want to put you in an awkward position."

Teddy waved his hands. "Diffuse it, Marcel. Tell him I am *not* interested in going. I just wanted to know."

"It's all right," Marcel said into the phone. "My friend does *not* want an invitation. He was just curious." Marcel quickly ended the call and turned to Teddy. "What's that all about?"

Teddy shook his head ruefully. "I forgot for a moment you're his boss. He takes a casual question as an order, but I don't want to alert anybody involved with the conference that I am poking around. I was just curious. Don't let me spoil a fine meal."

"Perhaps another cognac would ease the tension?"

Teddy smiled. "I like how you think."

As they finished the meal, Teddy said, "Now then, I have no intention of going to this panel, but I would love to see where it is taking place."

45.

THE CONFERENCE ROOM where the invitation-only panel would be held was pretty much what Teddy had expected. It differed very little from the other conference rooms at the convention, except those rooms were nestled next to each other and often featured temporary walls that could be slid back to merge two small panel rooms into one larger panel room, or four small panel rooms into an even larger panel room.

The conference room was self-contained. All walls were solid. There was no window. Unlike the double doors that opened into the other panel rooms, it had one single, solid door with a fairly substantial-looking lock. Teddy figured it might take him as much as a minute to open it.

"So what do you think?" Marcel said.

"Mind if I try a little experiment?" Teddy said.

"No, not at all. Be my guest."

"Go in, close the door, and have a conversation. Talk to Stone and Dino at a normal level, then talk like someone speaking on a panel. Will they be using microphones, Marcel?"

"In a room this size, I doubt it. We would supply them, if asked. Do you want me to find out if any have been requested?"

"No, that won't be necessary. But let's make this test."

Teddy went out and they closed the door. He waited a minute, but heard nothing. Finally he knocked on the door.

Marcel opened it with an inquiring look. "Well?"

"Perfect," Teddy said. "You can't hear a thing."

"And that's good?"

"It's good for the security of the panel room. I quite approve. If I ever need to hold a secret meeting, I'd be happy to have it here."

Marcel walked them back to the lobby and said good night to his guests.

"Now then," Teddy said, as Marcel was walking away. "If you don't mind, I'll meet you back at the house."

Stone frowned. "You have something to do?"

"I hope not," Teddy said.

GLENVILLE WAS WATCHING the front door when Stone and Dino emerged. He grabbed his cell phone and texted: Other two left, not the target.

Aziz could see that for himself. Since leaving Glenville, he had worked his way around the building and climbed a tree that commanded a view of the entrance. He texted back: Circle hotel.

Glenville sighed. It was another case where he'd like clarification. He assumed what Aziz meant was to check all the exits to see if Barnett had gone out another door. He hurried to do that.

A side door opened, and a man came out. He wasn't their quarry, but he was clearly a guest who was dining or staying at the hotel.

Glenville texted Aziz: Found one side exit, checking for others.

THROUGH THE SLIGHTEST crack in the side exit door, Teddy watched Glenville's shadow continue around the building. Then he slipped out the door, and headed in the opposite direction.

Teddy spotted Aziz in the tree just before he fired. That alone saved him. The little man impressed him as someone who did not miss. The rifle had a silencer, and the only sound was the whine of the bullet caroming off the side of the building.

Teddy ruined his assailant's aim by doing the one thing a shooter wouldn't expect. He charged straight at him. He ducked to the side, dived into a somersault, and came up behind a potted bush.

He couldn't see it, but Teddy could feel the rifle swinging in his direction. His gun was in his hand, he had drawn it as he rolled. He fired in the direction from which he judged the shot to have come. A yelp told him he was on target.

There was no clatter from a dropped rifle. The sniper was still armed. A moment later a crash and grunt told the story. The sniper had decided to climb down and fell.

He still had his gun, but he'd lost the advantage of surprise. And a rifle was a clumsy weapon for fighting up close.

Teddy shortened the distance between them. He could make out the stocky profile as the little man struggled to his feet.

At that moment, the other man charged Teddy from the side. His shadow wasn't much of a threat, but the little man was rushing him, too, and he couldn't take them both at once. He had to shoot one of them. He wanted to keep the little man alive.

Teddy shot his shadow in the head. No wounding, no warning shot, Teddy put him out of the way to go after his prize.

The little man seemed to sense it was a real possibility that Teddy might put him out of action and capture him alive. Teddy was sure the little man didn't want that to happen. Somehow it would be worse than being shot dead.

Teddy was right. The little man backed into the darkness, even with Teddy's gun trained on him.

Teddy could have shot him.

He sighed.

He probably should have.

46.

TEDDY RETURNED TO Stone's house to find him and Dino having a nightcap.

"I thought we lost you," Dino said.

"You almost did."

"What?"

"A minor incident. But would you guys mind leaving tomorrow?"

"What!" Dino said.

"Just how minor *was* this incident?" Stone asked.

"Well, let me put it this way. I'm glad we left by separate doors."

"Just what happened?" Stone said.

"What happened that we have to leave tomorrow?" Dino said. "I was just beginning to enjoy the place."

"And I have a dinner date," Stone said.

"Why am I not surprised?" Teddy said. "I'm afraid something has come up."

"Oh?"

"I sort of killed someone."

"'Sort of'?" Stone said.

Dino put up his hand. "This is not the type of thing you tell a police commissioner."

"You have jurisdiction in France?"

"Good point."

"Is that why we have to leave?" Stone said. "Because you accomplished your purpose and you're going home?"

"Not at all," Teddy said. "The man I killed is not the man who was trying to kill me."

"You shot an innocent bystander?" Dino said.

"He's a member of the opposition, but he wasn't the hit man. And he wasn't the mole I was sent here to find."

"If he's not the man, why are you leaving?"

"Well, that's the thing." Teddy said.

"Uh-oh. You're not leaving, you're just sending us home? Is this for our own protection?"

"No, and I didn't say I wasn't leaving."

"You *are* leaving?"

"I'm getting on the plane with you."

"Why does that not sound like the same thing?" Dino said.

"Agent Felix Dressler must go home. Too many people are interested in him, and it's rendered him ineffective. So, for all intents and purposes, I'm leaving with you tomorrow." Teddy looked at Stone. "Do you have Internet service here?"

"Of course. Why?"

"I need to send an e-mail."

Teddy sat down at Stone's computer and sent an encoded e-mail to Lance: Belt is buckled. Coming home.

"Can't they break that code?" Stone said.

"I'm sure they can."

"Then they'll know it was sent from my computer."

"Yes, which will fit in nicely with my leaving with you tomorrow." Teddy got up from the desk. "Now, do you mind if I borrow your car?"

"Of course you can borrow my car. Where are you going?"

"To send an e-mail."

TEDDY DROVE TO the nearest hotel and used the computer in the lobby to send an encrypted message to Millie.

He also sent an encrypted message to Kevin. That message was brief:

a) Melvin Melbourne; b) Daniel Remington; c) Arnold
Mycroft; d) Claude Fisher. Send only lowercase
letter.

Teddy logged off the computer, drove back to the mews house, and returned the car keys to Stone.

"All right, gentlemen, the bait is in the trap. All systems are go. We need to be all packed and ready to leave for the airport at three o'clock tomorrow. We need to be sure the plane is fueled up and ready to go."

"That goes without saying," Stone said.

"But there's a wrinkle," Teddy said.

"Oh?"

"There are a few extra preparations for this particular flight."

"Like what?"

Teddy held up one finger. "Okay," he said, "here's what I need."

JORAM GLANCED UP from his computer. He had news, but he wanted to tread lightly. Aziz had texted: Target alive. Glenville dead. Fahd, understandably, was in a mood.

"Sir," Joram said. "I have intercepted an e-mail."

"What e-mail?" Fahd said.

"An e-mail to Lance Cabot, sent from Stone Barrington's computer."

"Stone Barrington e-mailed Lance Cabot?"

"Apparently not. The e-mail originated from his computer, but the e-mail is signed 'Felix.' Isn't that the name Billy Barnett has been using?"

"What did the e-mail say?"

"'Belt is buckled. Coming home.'"

Fahd frowned.

"What does it mean?" Fahd said.

"I'm not sure. I'll keep watch. See what else comes in."

Fahd went back to his desk and sat, thinking. He was not at all convinced. "Belt is buckled"? What did that mean? Presumably that Billy Barnett had done the job. Could he possibly think Glenville was the mole, that taking him out solved the problem? No, Glenville didn't work for the CIA. He was a hired thug, plain and simple—and not a particularly good one. So why was Billy Barnett going home?

Fahd didn't care why, so long as he actually left. This e-mail was no real indication. He needed proof.

Fahd texted Aziz: Target may be leaving town. Be alert for trip to airport. Good if he leaves, but verify.

47.

I N THE MORNING Teddy checked in with Jacques at the café.

Jacques was apologetic. "I did the best I could. There are three American big-game hunters scheduled to attend the panel. One is in Seattle, one is in Miami. Both are flying to Paris on the same day they are checking into l'Arrington. They have no side excursions before that.

"The third is Floyd Maitland of Dallas, Texas. He flew out two days ago and is currently vacationing at a beach on the Mediterranean."

"Where?"

"In Nice."

"He's already in France?"

"Yes. He plans to stay there until his flight to Paris."

Teddy smiled. "Interesting. Do you have a picture?"

Jacques swung the laptop around and showed him. "Maitland is a stereotypical Texan with a handlebar moustache and a Stetson hat."

"Does he always wear that hat, or just for photos?"

"I googled him and got this."

Jacques called up the images he'd saved. Apparently

Maitland always wore the hat, even in the candid shots. Blue jeans and a leather belt with a large buckle completed the picture.

"I don't suppose you have a recording of his voice?"

Jacques clicked on video and played a YouTube clip of Maitland addressing a dinner crowd of cattle ranchers.

"Tell me something. Does Maitland seem like a good guy, aside from his desire to kill defenseless animals?"

"Not at all. He's an oilman, but he's rumored to have made as much money trafficking undocumented immigrants to work as slaves on farms, in factories, or worse. A very bad man."

Teddy nodded his approval. "Listen, Jacques, I've been called home. I'll be leaving today."

"Is anything wrong?"

"Just bureaucratic bullshit. I hope to be back. Be alert for an encrypted e-mail."

48.

MILLIE MET Lance Cabot in front of the Washington Monument.

"Is this really necessary?" Lance said.

"Our friend thinks so," Millie said. Millie was in plain clothes and could have passed as a CIA agent. Lance wondered if that was what she was angling for.

"Why? The mission is over. He's on his way home."

"He e-mailed you directly?"

"That's right." Lance's face fell. "Oh, shit."

Millie smiled. "You figured there was no need for back channels because the job was done, which is just what he wanted it to look like. Here's the real message: He hasn't found the mole yet, but he's working on it. He hopes to have results soon."

"Oh, he does, does he? What progress has he made?"

"He didn't say. He just wanted to alert you to the fact that the mole may be the least of our problems."

Lance's mouth fell open. "A mole working inside the CIA is 'the least of our problems'? What could be worse than that?"

"He didn't specify, but he thinks it's something big."

"He told you nothing specific?"

"He did say people were trying to kill him."

"I know how they feel," Lance said. "He didn't tell you anything about whatever it is that he thinks is more important than the job *I* sent him to do there?"

"I'm afraid not."

"Did he tell you anything about the attempts on his life?"

"He said they failed."

"No kidding. Tell me, is he actually working on this, or is he just having fun?"

"He says: 'It's not fun, it's hard work and it's dangerous—and stop griping about it and giving Millie a hard time.'"

"He didn't say that."

"Yes, he did."

"He anticipated the question?"

"Word for word." Millie cocked her head. "Kind of makes you want to trust his instincts, don't you think?"

49.

TEDDY HAD TEXTED Kristin, Tied up tonight, see you tomorrow. He figured as a CIA agent she should accept that as a matter of course.

As a woman, he figured, she probably wouldn't.

He figured right.

"Big night last night?" Kristin said, when Teddy checked in at the embassy.

Teddy shrugged. "Average. I'm making progress."

"With whom?"

"A fat Russian spy. He was playing hard to get, but I lured him with my cypher code."

Kristin laughed. "You're terrible."

He took her out to lunch and tried to prepare her for what was to come. "I'll be leaving soon. I may not have a chance to say goodbye."

She frowned. "Leaving? Why?"

"I'm not my own man. I go where they tell me."

"And they're telling you to leave?"

"They will."

"How do you know?"

"I have a feel for these things."

"Is it because of the men who tried to mug us?"

"That was just an isolated incident."

"You're lying to me."

"I wouldn't lie to you."

"Will you be back?"

"I go where they send me."

"Where are they sending you now?"

"They haven't told me yet. I just know I'll be moving on."

"Why are you so infuriating?"

"It's the nature of the job."

Their parting was civil but strained. Kristin went back to her office. Teddy made an excuse not to go back with her, not wishing to continue the conversation.

He also wanted to see if he was being followed.

He was, but it wasn't one of the bad guys. It was Agent Workman from the CIA station. That was interesting. Workman had followed him before, found everything there was to find. So why was he tailing Teddy again now?

Despite what Kristin had said, Teddy thought the young agent had feelings for her; in which case, he had to resent the hell out of Teddy.

Teddy led Agent Workman in a neutral direction, neither toward the embassy nor toward his apartment, just to see if he'd tag along. He did. Teddy found that interesting.

Teddy went into the first hotel he came to, to give the young man a thrill, and to check in on the computer. He logged on with no real expectations, and discovered an encrypted e-mail from Kevin. It read in its entirety:

c).

The notation "c)" was assigned to Arnold Mycroft.

Someone had run an Internet search for Arnold Mycroft.

Arnold Mycroft was the name on the passport Workman had seen in the locker.

Teddy debated sending an e-mail to Millie, but decided he didn't have time.

He left the hotel and spotted Workman down the block. There was still no sign of the assassin from the night before. Teddy set off down the street. If the little hit man was around, he'd have to show himself.

As Teddy walked, he could spot no one following but Workman. Perfect. Teddy reacted as if his cell phone had just rung. He jerked it out of his pocket and pretended to answer the call. He nodded, and slipped the phone back in his pocket.

Teddy looked around. He was near a small café.

A row of cars were parked down the side street. One of them—an older model—had its driver's-side window down. Teddy walked up to it as if he owned it, opened the door, and got in.

The keys were not in the ignition, but Teddy had no trouble hot-wiring the car. He backed up and pulled out of the alley. As he turned the corner, he could see Agent Workman run out into the middle of the street hailing a cab.

Teddy drove out of town. Occasionally he could see Agent Workman's taxi following in the distance. He wasn't worried that he might lose him. Workman was a trained agent.

TEDDY CAME TO a small vineyard a few miles out of town. It looked like a family-run place. Teddy could envision mom and pop tending the vines, and their sixteen-year-old daughter, barefoot with her skirt hiked up, trampling the grapes. The bottles would have hand-lettered labels dating back at least a century, and passed on from generation to generation.

The stomping tub was in evidence, though no one was in it. They were probably all out in the field.

It didn't matter. Teddy was reacting to a nonexistent cell phone message. He headed for the barn as if that was where he had been told to go.

The first room was full of wine bottles. They were empty, unused, and without labels. Most were in partitioned cardboard cases, but some had been unpacked onto rickety metal shelves.

Teddy pushed on farther into the barn. He found a couple of livestock stalls for either cows or horses. None were evident.

At the far end of the barn, where one would least expect it, was a business office, complete with phone, fax, and computer. That took Teddy aback. He couldn't recall seeing electricity coming into the barn. Either he was slipping, or the wires were underground.

Teddy sat down at the computer and opened their e-mail. He pulled up a message at random and pretended to decode it. He grabbed a pencil and a piece of paper and with quick strokes, glancing back and forth between the computer and his writing, he "translated" the message, which read: Enemy wise. Ditch cover.

Teddy could hear the creak of floorboards in the barn. Workman was being careful, but there was no way to walk on that wooden floor without giving himself away.

Teddy sat at the desk and kept up the facade of decoding. He could feel Workman's eyes on him, but no weapon. A weapon trained on him always put him on high alert. If pressed, Teddy could not say how he knew, but he did.

There was a bathroom off the office, at least a half bath with toilet and sink. Teddy got up, switched on the light, went inside, and closed the door. He could visualize Workman creeping toward the desk.

Teddy gave him ten seconds and then came out with his gun drawn.

Workman was bent over the desk, reading what Teddy had written from the e-mail. At the sound of the door, he glanced up in alarm and saw the man with the gun.

"You shouldn't have reported the name on the passport, Workman," Teddy said.

"What are you talking about?"

"You followed me home. You searched my flat. You followed me to the train station. You searched my locker. You're a professional. You didn't take any of my money, but you did look at my passport."

Workman gave up the pretense. "Who are you really? What are you doing here?"

"Looking for you."

Teddy gestured toward the door and, knowing he was beat, Workman began walking. Teddy followed behind, his gun still at the ready.

They were almost to the door when Workman suddenly spun around and chopped down on Teddy's gun hand. It would have worked on most men. With Teddy, Workman was lucky to graze his arm.

Teddy was hoping for such a move. It would cut through pretense and shorten the discussion. Only Workman was no slouch. Even as he missed with his first move, he was drawing his own gun with his other hand.

Teddy wasn't surprised. Risking exposure, the mole would have to kill him. There would be no middle ground, no wound and interrogate. Workman would go for the kill.

Teddy shot first.

TEDDY SEARCHED WORKMAN'S body. He found nothing of interest, nothing that would indicate that he was anything other than a CIA agent.

Teddy knew better.

He left Agent Workman in a horse stall, covered up with hay. With luck, the family wouldn't find him until the body started to stink.

50.

TEDDY FOUND WORKMAN'S cab waiting outside the vineyard gate. He paid off the driver and told him his buddy had decided to go back to town with him.

Teddy drove the stolen car back to town, dropped it off near the café, and stopped in at the embassy. Kristin didn't seem to be around, which was a blessing. He didn't want to go through that scene again. He checked in with Norton, and told him he had to leave.

"So soon?" Norton said.

Teddy grinned. "Yeah, I know you'll miss me. The fact is, there's nothing for me to do here, and the powers that be are pulling me out."

"Well, I can't pretend I'm sorry to hear it. Nothing against you personally, but one hates to have one's department under review."

Teddy shrugged and shook his head. "See, that's the problem. There's absolutely no way you can tell someone whose department *isn't* under review that they're not under review. Give my regards to the rest of the gang. A fine bunch, as far as I can tell. I'm sorry to see them so briefly and under such awkward circumstances."

Teddy shook hands with Norton, and went out.

This time the little man *was* following him. He was scrunched down in the front seat of a car. Teddy wasn't surprised. With Workman and the other spy gone, the Syrians must be running short of personnel.

The little man wasn't trying to shoot him this time, just keeping him under surveillance. Teddy figured they must have decoded the e-mail. Plus, they hadn't yet heard about Workman.

Teddy hailed a cab and took it back to his apartment, the one everyone knew about. He packed a suitcase, turned off the light, and went out.

The hit man was lurking on the corner. He was short and stocky, and had a hard time hiding. Clearly he was a much better hit man than a stalker.

Teddy hailed a cab and took it to Stone's mews house.

The little man climbed into his car and followed behind.

Teddy paid off his cab and lugged in his suitcase, being careful to make sure the little man was only watching. There was always the chance he might try to shorten his day by getting off a shot.

Stone's and Dino's bags were in the foyer. Teddy added his to the row, and went in to find them enjoying one last drink.

"All set?" Teddy asked.

"All except for your gear," Stone said. "I figured you'd rather take it out of the safe yourself than have it lying there in the foyer."

"Excellent. Well, finish your drinks and we'll head out."

"You're not in a hurry?" Dino said.

Teddy grinned. "It's a private plane. It leaves when we do."

Teddy sat down and told them about his day. He left out killing Workman. That was something Lance needed to hear first.

When they'd finished their drinks, Stone opened the safe and Teddy grabbed his gear.

Stone buzzed Hugo, the gardener, handyman, and caretaker, who lived in the small apartment over the garage. He was driving them to the airport, and came down to help them load their bags into the car.

"Keep your heads down as we go out the gate," Teddy said. "I don't expect anyone to take a shot at us, but it would be a hell of a way to end the trip."

No one fired at them. The little man was in his car down the block. When they pulled out of the driveway, he tagged along.

The drive was uneventful. The little man kept up with them until they went through the airport gate. Then he drove parallel to them along the side road, keeping them in sight.

The Strategic Services jet was standing out in front of the hangar. Hugo drove up to it and helped them unload the car. They shook hands with him, and he drove off.

Men came out of the hangar and helped them carry their bags to the plane. When they were finished, Stone tipped them and thanked them. They were immediately replaced by mechanics and servicemen who swarmed over the plane, checking every last inch.

Stone, Teddy, and Dino boarded the plane while this was going on.

"Where are my supplies?" Teddy asked.

"Right this way," Stone said, grabbing Teddy's suitcase. Teddy hoisted his equipment bag and followed along.

Stone led them to a private room in the rear of the plane.

On the desk were a mechanic's toolkit and gear bag. There was also a uniform, identical to the ones the mechanics servicing the plane were wearing.

Teddy changed quickly into the mechanic's outfit. With the cap on, he didn't even have to alter his appearance. He quickly unpacked his equipment bag. He put his makeup in the toolkit, along with his money, passports, credentials, and burner phones. He put his wigs and weapons in the gear bag.

He popped open the suitcase and added the few personal items he needed. Having the second secret apartment allowed him to travel very light.

Teddy checked his appearance in the mirror. He touched it up slightly, adding a grease smear, and he was good to go. He said goodbye to Stone and Dino, and joined the group of similarly dressed mechanics getting off the plane.

AZIZ WASN'T TAKING anything for granted. He saw the men board the plane, and he stuck around to make sure it took off.

He was not surprised by the swarm of mechanics.

Anyone savvy enough to have foiled two assassination attempts would be alert to the possibility of someone sabotaging the plane.

Aziz wished he'd thought to do it. Of course, it had never occurred to him that his target would still be alive.

Finally the mechanics finished their inspection and filed off the plane. The ramp was pulled away and the door closed. After what seemed an interminable time, the plane roared to life, pulled away, and taxied down the runway.

Aziz stood watching until it actually took off. Only then did he pull out his cell phone and text: He's gone.

51.

TEDDY TOOK A car service back from the airport. He got out two blocks away from the apartment no one knew about and lugged his equipment the rest of the way. He locked the door behind him and threw the bag on the bed. He stripped off his airplane mechanic's work clothes, went in the bathroom, and washed up. It took a while to get off all the grease and grime.

When he was done, he dug into his equipment bag and sorted through his IDs. Dino had rented the apartment for him under the name Fenton Towne, but he didn't want to be Fenton Towne at the moment. He selected Devon Billingham, a bit of a mouthful, but an identity with a passport photo different enough from his current guise as Felix Dressler that no one would notice the resemblance.

Teddy got his makeup kit out of the equipment bag, went in the bathroom, and changed his appearance to match the photo on Devon Billingham's passport. When he was satisfied with the result he dressed himself in a pair of loafers, casual slacks, and a polo shirt. Felix Dressler had worn a suit. Such a simple thing as a different choice of attire would go a long way toward preventing an inadvertent recognition.

Teddy went out to a luggage store and bought a suitcase and a small steamer trunk with a substantial combination lock. The owner was happy to take Devon Billingham's credit card. It was perfectly valid and checked out when the owner ran it, as would any of Teddy's phony credit cards.

The salesman helped Teddy carry the suitcase and trunk out to a taxi. This time Teddy had the cab take him right to the door of his apartment. There was no danger in doing so, as Devon Billingham.

Teddy tipped the cabbie to carry the trunk upstairs—enough that he'd be happy, but not so much that he would tell all his friends.

The moment the cabbie was gone, Teddy locked the door behind him and checked under the bed. The equipment bag was right where he'd left it. He had known it would be. It had only been an hour. Still, he was never comfortable leaving his equipment unsecured.

Now Teddy placed the equipment bag in the steamer trunk, locked it, and set the combination. He put the suitcase on the bed and packed what few clothes he had. There weren't many.

He called the Hôtel St. Pierre and made a reservation for the week, starting immediately. He called for a cab, met it on the street, and had the cabbie come up and help him with the luggage. He took the cab to the St. Pierre, checked in, and let the bellboy bring the bags up to the room.

As soon as the bellboy had left, Teddy unlocked the trunk, took out the equipment bag, and selected only the essentials he was likely to use, such as his makeup kit, Devon Billingham's IDs, and Felix Dressler's credentials. He took a few burner phones, a gun with a silencer, and a shoulder holster. The rest he locked back up in the trunk.

He called the front desk and had a bellboy bring up a luggage cart for the trunk. He took it down to the front desk and asked to see the manager. The desk clerk made a call, and within minutes a bald, bespectacled well-dressed man bustled up to the desk and asked if there was anything he could do.

"Actually, there is," Teddy said. "Devon Billingham. I deal in antique jewelry, the rarest of the rare. I am here from the States in pursuit of a few elusive pieces that I have had my eye on for some time. I wish to use your hotel as my base of operations. I have rented a room for the week, but I will not be here every night. Should the chambermaid report that my bed has not been slept in, please do not panic and notify the authorities or institute a search to see if I have given up the room. I haven't. So there can be no mistake, I am paying my entire bill in advance, at least the room charge for the seven days. Is that acceptable to you?"

"But of course, monsieur."

"If you could please convey these instructions to your staff so that I am not bothered by any nonsense while I am here, I would appreciate it."

"I assure you, it will be taken care of."

"Thank you." Teddy stepped aside and indicated the cart. "I have already made some valuable acquisitions. Can you be responsible for placing my trunk in safe-keeping?"

"I will place it in the hotel safe." The manager cleared his throat. "When you say 'responsible,' we can keep your trunk undisturbed, but you understand the hotel cannot be held liable for any jewelry that you may claim was in the trunk."

"But of course," Teddy said, palming the man a fifty-euro note. "I trust you to handle this discreetly. There is no reason for anyone to know how valuable the contents of the trunk actually are."

The manager beamed. "There certainly is not."

TEDDY WENT OUT to a sporting goods store that specialized in camping gear and outdoor wear. He bought some denim shirts, blue jeans, and a wide leather belt with a large silver buckle. He bought the largest duffel bag he could find, a coil of rope, a hunting knife, plastic bags of various sizes, and extra-large twist ties.

The clerk directed him to a specialty store where he found a pair of cowboy boots and a Stetson hat, as well as a western gun belt and holster.

"Costume party?" the salesclerk asked.

Teddy grinned. "Doesn't everyone dress like this?"

Teddy brought his purchases back to the hotel. He dined in his room while he sorted and packed. He went to bed early, awoke at eight, and caught a flight to Nice.

He took a cab to Sur la Mer, a seaside hotel, and checked in as Devon Billingham.

"Just the one night?" the clerk asked.

"Wish I could stay," Teddy said ruefully. "I'm meeting a friend of mine. Floyd Maitland. Has he checked in yet?"

The desk clerk consulted his computer. "Two days ago."

"I don't suppose you could tell me the room number."

The clerk smiled. "It is not done."

"I understand. May I leave him a note?"

"But of course."

Teddy took a piece of note paper, scrawled: *Floyd. I'm here. Call me. Devon.* He folded it up, wrote *Floyd Maitland* on it, and gave it to the desk clerk. "Can you see that he gets it?"

"Yes, of course."

As he turned to go, Teddy could see the desk clerk putting his note in box 432.

52.

FLOYD MAITLAND LEANED back in his beach chair and stroked his luxurious moustache. Floyd loved the beach, though it was hard to maintain his image there. He couldn't wear his Stetson with a bathing suit. On the other hand, he could enjoy tall, cool mixed drinks with little umbrellas in them. In a Texas barroom, he wouldn't be caught dead drinking anything but straight bourbon.

The blond waitress, in the skimpy bikini that Maitland liked, padded by in the sand. He waved to her. She nodded at him, but stopped to take the order of two young Frenchmen in beach chairs. He could see her laughing and flirting with them.

He bawled her out when she took his order. Some nerve. She was supposed to be bending over *him* and giggling in that flimsy top.

He had another wicked frozen concoction.

By the time Maitland left the beach he was quite loaded, which wasn't fair somehow. He knew exactly how much bourbon he could drink. These mixed drinks snuck up on a fellow.

Maitland went back to his room, hopped in the shower to wash away the sand, and dressed for dinner. It took a little longer than if he hadn't been drinking all afternoon, but a half hour later he was fully decked out in a denim shirt, blue jeans, and cowboy boots, a casual ensemble that cost more than the monthly salary of one of his farmhands. He put on his Stetson hat and looked in the full-length mirror. He cut a dashing figure, if he did say so himself. He hoped that the little brunette he'd been talking to the night before would be in the bar. Of course, in the bar he'd have to go back to bourbon. How would that mix?

There was a knock on the door.

Maitland frowned. He hadn't called room service. Surely he would remember that. Perhaps it was the little brunette. He'd given her his room number. No, it would be the bellboy with some annoying message or other.

Maitland crossed the room, not staggering, but very aware of where he was putting his feet. He opened the door and gawked.

Staring back at him was . . .

Floyd Maitland!

It was like looking in a mirror.

What the hell?

"Take off your hat."

Maitland blinked stupidly. "What?"

"Take off your hat," the man said, raising his own Stetson.

Maitland blindly mimicked him, raising his hat.

Before Maitland had a chance to realize what was happening, his doppelgänger aimed a gun at his head. It was an automatic. It had a long barrel. A silencer.

Maitland had time to think, *That's not my gun*, before it shot him in the head.

53.

Teddy stepped into Maitland's room and closed the door. Maitland had done him the favor of falling over backward so Teddy didn't have to move the body to do so.

Teddy grabbed a DO NOT DISTURB sign off the inside knob, opened the door, slipped it on the outside knob, and retrieved the duffel bag he'd left in the hallway. This time he closed and locked the door.

Teddy grabbed a towel from the bathroom and slipped it under Maitland's head. He dug into the duffel bag and came out with a plastic bag about the size of a wastepaper basket liner. He slipped it around Maitland's head and sealed it with a twist tie.

Maitland's Stetson had fallen on the rug. Teddy picked it up and examined it. The hat was old and weather-beaten, clearly the man's favorite. Maitland would take pride in the fact that it was worn, proof that despite his wealth and habits he wasn't all hat and no cattle.

Teddy searched the body. Maitland's wallet was in the hip pocket of his jeans. It contained a driver's license, several credit cards, and various other cards, including a membership in the NRA.

Teddy continued searching the body, but found nothing else of value. The clothes, however, were another story. Maitland's denim jacket had clearly been tailor-made and looked stylish, if such a term applied to western wear. It had seemed fairly snug on Maitland, and Teddy figured it would fit him. He stripped it off, being careful that no blood was leaking from the plastic bag.

Teddy also took off Maitland's boots. They were ornate, and made out of what appeared to be the skin of a diamondback rattlesnake. He figured Maitland had a story about their provenance, probably apocryphal.

Maitland's belt, though of seasoned leather and adorned with a gaudy buckle, had unfortunately been let out a few times to accommodate the man's girth. With Teddy's slimmer waist, the worn holes would be noticeable. Teddy stripped it off nonetheless.

Teddy hadn't found what he was looking for, but a leather briefcase on the coffee table looked promising. He sat down and popped it open. His search was immediately rewarded. In a small outer compartment were Maitland's airline ticket and passport. That was a stroke of luck. The trip to Paris was a domestic flight. No passport would be needed, but now he had it just in case.

Now for the body.

Teddy dumped everything out of the duffel bag and laid it out next to Maitland on the floor. It was a couple of feet short. Teddy knew it would be. That was why he had brought the duct tape.

Teddy stripped off Maitland's pants, not that he wanted them, just to make the body easier to deal with. He folded his legs at the knee, and taped his ankles to his thighs with duct tape. It was not a particularly neat job, but that didn't matter. Maitland was now short enough to fit in the duffel bag. Teddy stuffed him in and zipped it shut.

Teddy called the front desk. "This is Floyd Maitland. My car's in valet parking. Could you have it brought around to the front in fifteen minutes? . . . Number? What number? . . . Oh, the number on the stub. It's one-four-three . . . Yes. And could you send a bellboy with a luggage cart up to my room?"

Teddy met the bellboy at the door. He palmed him a bill and said, "Wait here." He pushed the cart into the room, closing the door, and heaved the duffel bag up on the cart. Maitland was heavy, and Teddy could have used the help, but he didn't want the bellboy to notice how much like a body his luggage actually was.

Teddy let the bellboy push the cart into the elevator and take it out front where a car was already waiting. Teddy smiled. He had expected the Texan to drive some huge, gas-guzzling Cadillac, but of course it was a rental of European proportions. The trunk was barely big enough to hold the duffel.

Teddy took the car keys from the valet and popped the trunk. The valet started to help with the bag, but Teddy waved him away.

"It's fragile and valuable. If it breaks, I don't want to be blaming you."

Teddy hefted the duffel into the trunk and slammed it shut. He handed bills to the bellboy and the valet, hopped in the car, and drove off.

It was not a scenic drive. Teddy did not follow the seashore, or take in any of the well-advertised tourist spots. Instead, he took a tour of alleys and back lots, searching for a likely dumpster in which to dump the body. He found none that was either large or full enough for the duffel to go unnoticed by the garbage men.

Finally Teddy gave up and went back to the hotel. He drove up to the door, handed the keys to the valet, and told him to park it.

Maitland would have to spend the night in the garage.

54.

AZIZ FELT HE'D failed, which indeed he had. Yet he gave no sign. He stood before Fahd, stolid as ever, awaiting the strongman's wrath.

It did not come. Perversely, Fahd seemed quite satisfied with the situation.

"So," he said, "we are all set. The man who was causing so much trouble has left Paris, and has no reason to come back. When we arrive the day after tomorrow, no one will be there to bother us. You will be on high alert, of course, but I do not expect any trouble. The men in our party are wonderful camouflage. We will seem like any other members of the convention."

Fahd looked at Aziz for approval and reassurance. Of course, he got none. He knew he wouldn't, but every now and then he couldn't help looking anyway.

Fahd scooped up the phone and barked, "Joram!"

The little computer technician poked his head in the door. "Sir?"

"Joram, I need you in this chair. Why are you not in this chair?"

"Sir, you told me to go. You were meeting with the general and you did not want me present."

"Well, I am not meeting him now, am I? Do you have my itinerary for Paris, as I requested?"

"Yes, sir." Joram sat at the computer and began typing.

"What are you doing?"

"Calling it up."

"I don't want to stand here reading over your shoulder. Print it out for me."

"Yes, sir." Joram did so, and handed it to him. "Our reservation is for you, Aziz, Dr. Habib, Dr. Chaim, and Dr. Badim. You're all registered for the conference, and you paid extra for the special panel: Rarest of the Rare. The three doctors have airline tickets. You and Aziz will be traveling by private plane."

"Where are the airline tickets?"

"I will print out the reservations. The boarding passes I can print out twenty-four hours before the flight."

"Can they get their own boarding passes at the airport?"

"Yes."

"Good. I suppose even doctors can figure out how to do that."

"They've been given instructions and a travel itinerary. They understand that you will brief them on what you want them to do."

"Oh, they understand that, do they?"

"They have been told."

"Then I suppose I have to do it."

Joram felt like somehow he had done something wrong. "Do you want me to do it for you?" he offered as a conciliatory gesture.

"You wouldn't know what to say. No, get them in here."

"Do you want them all at once?"

"Three scientists? I'd never keep them straight. One at a time, please."

Joram sat down and started making calls.

55.

D R. HABIB WAS concerned. He'd been delighted when he learned he was going to a rare animal convention in Paris. Less so when he learned he would be attending with Fahd, a reputed military strongman and weapons dealer, a man with no background or interest in zoology. Fahd's attendance at a conservation convention did not compute, but his orders were clear. He was to report to Fahd and receive his instructions for the trip to Paris. So he was nervous when he knocked on the door.

The door was opened by a short, stocky man with a bald head. That would be Aziz. Dr. Habib had heard stories about Aziz. He hoped they weren't true.

Aziz motioned Dr. Habib in, so that story at least was accurate. The little man was mute.

Fahd was seated behind his desk. He did not get up to greet the doctor, or offer him a chair. He just let him stand there while he finished up some paperwork.

Finally he looked up.

"And you are?"

"Dr. Habib."

Fahd consulted a paper on his desk. "Yes. You will be going to the rare animal convention in Paris."

"Yes, sir."

"As a zoologist, you must be pleased."

"I am."

"You don't sound pleased."

"I *am* pleased. I'm just somewhat confused. Why am I going?"

"You're going to study animals. Isn't that what zoologists do?"

"Yes, of course. I'm going with Dr. Chaim and Dr. Badim."

"How do you know that?"

"I asked."

Fahd glanced over at Joram. The computer technician was suddenly very busy studying the desktop monitor.

Dr. Habib found he could not resist a little subtle digging for information. He affected a casual mien. "Dr. Badim is a microbiologist. I wonder why he is going."

"To study the animals, of course."

"Yes. I'm just concerned that he is a microbiologist. If there is any infectious disease we are on the lookout for, it would be of some concern. Particularly if it was common to any specific breed of animal."

"I assure you there is not."

"It is strange, though."

"Will this prevent you from having a good time?"

"No."

Fahd cocked his head. "Joram, would you mind working in the other room? I would like to talk to Dr. Habib alone. Someone seems to be telling people our business."

"Yes, sir. Right away, sir."

Joram got up and scuttled out.

"Now then," Fahd said, getting up from his chair and walking around the desk. "I would like to allay your doubts about our project. If you have doubts, you will not have a good time." Fahd put his arm around Dr. Habib's shoulders. "I'm going to let you talk to Professor Malik. He is an expert in the field, and can explain the need for a microbiologist. I assure you it is nothing sinister. Aziz, would you please take Dr. Habib and introduce him to Professor Malik. Tell him he has my authority to speak freely about the conference."

Fahd made a face. "What am I saying? Of course you can't tell him. He's a mute, you see. Here. Take him this note."

Fahd went to the desk, pulled a piece of paper from a pocket notebook, and wrote *Kill him* on it. He folded it up and handed it to Aziz.

Aziz nodded, and led Dr. Habib out.

Fahd picked up the phone and barked, "Joram!"

Joram expected to be in serious trouble for telling the doctor who else was going with him to Paris. "Yes, sir," he said meekly.

"Change the itinerary. We're only taking two doctors."

56.

TEDDY WOKE UP and called the front desk from his cell. "This is Devon Billingham in room three oh eight. I'm checking out. My bill's paid, and I'm leaving my keys in the room."

Teddy wasn't in Devon's room. He was upstairs in Floyd Maitland's suite, and he didn't feel like dressing up like Devon Billingham just to check out. He'd already left the keys and taken his suitcase, so he just had to make the phone call.

Teddy had breakfast, got Maitland's car back from valet parking, and drove down to the dock. He went into a bait-and-tackle shop and bought a fishing rod, a creel, a net, a beer cooler, and two extra-large coolers.

The salesclerk grinned and inquired in halting English, "You plan on catch that much?"

"If your equipment's any good," Teddy told him.

Teddy found the French equivalent of a Home Depot and bought two fifty-pound bags of cement. The salesman helped him carry them out. He headed for the trunk, but Teddy stopped him.

"Throw them in the backseat."

The salesman was surprised. "Really?"

"Trunk's full," Teddy told him.

After a couple of blocks Teddy stopped, got out, and poured the cement into the two large coolers. He crumpled up the bags and threw them in a garbage can on the street corner.

Teddy stopped at the first convenience store he came to and bought a bag of ice and two six packs of Bud Lite. He took them out to the car and filled the beer cooler.

Teddy got back in the car, drove down to a marina, and rented a boat. It was expensive—even more so because he didn't want a pilot. He had to sign a zillion forms exempting liability in the event anything happened. He signed them as Floyd Maitland. If he wrecked the boat, Teddy figured, Floyd was in a lot of trouble.

It was a while since Teddy had piloted a boat, but like riding a bicycle, Teddy didn't forget. A sailboat might have been trickier, but a cabin cruiser was a piece of cake. Teddy maneuvered easily through the harbor and headed for the open sea.

As soon as he was more or less alone he killed the motor, dropped anchor, and went to work.

First he took out the fishing rod, unwound the line, and cast it off the stern of the ship. He was terrible at casting, but no one was looking. He stuck the handle of the rod into one of the round metal holders built into the rail for that purpose. He left the net and the creel lying on the deck to complete the picture. He realized these were hollow gestures that would only fool the most casual inspection. There wasn't even bait on the hook.

Teddy popped open the beer cooler, grabbed a few cans, and poured them out in the sea. He popped another can, chugged half of it, and poured the rest out. He tossed the empty on the deck with the others, and turned his attention to the task at hand.

Teddy unzipped the duffel and took out his tools, which he had packed carefully around the body. He took out a roll of duct tape and taped up the coolers. They had latches, but Teddy wasn't about to trust them. He wound the duct tape around the coolers, taping them crosswise and lengthwise again and again.

When he was satisfied, he took out a coil of rope and fed it through the handles of the coolers. He tied it off with knots he knew would hold, whether they would have impressed a true seaman or not. He reinforced them with duct tape nonetheless.

He pulled Maitland out of the duffel bag. It would have been easier to leave him in the bag, but if the body was ever discovered, the duffel could conceivably be traced back to the sporting goods store where it was purchased by Devon Billingham. That could lead to complications.

Teddy tied the rope to Maitland. He tied his legs, his arms, his neck, and his body, each with a separate length of rope, so if one gave, the others wouldn't.

Teddy had just finished tying up the body when he noticed a boat bearing down on him. It was still in the distance, but it was coming fast. It was a police boat, and within minutes it would be close enough for them to see what he was doing.

There was nowhere to hide, not with a dead man lying faceup on the deck. Teddy stooped down, grabbed the coolers and, keeping low, heaved one after another over the side. Maitland's body skidded across the deck and disappeared in the deep.

That left Teddy sprawled out on the deck. His actions would seem incomprehensible to the police in the boat. They'd want to know what he was doing. He needed a useful prop. He lunged for the beer cooler, pulled out a can, and popped the top. Teddy staggered to his feet and careened in the direction of his fishing pole just as the police boat pulled up alongside.

Teddy waved and saluted them with a beer.

Whatever the police had been expecting, a drunken cowboy wasn't it. The police captain yelled something in French.

Teddy yelled back, "No speako le French!"

The policeman visibly rolled his eyes.

"Monsieur, have you been drinking?" the police captain asked.

Teddy looked surprised. He looked at the beer in his hand, then back at the officer. "No."

The officer stared at him.

Teddy laughed a hearty, good-ol'-boy Texan laugh. "I'm not drunk, just seasick. I love to fish, but I hate the water. And the water doesn't like me. I drink a little beer to take the edge off. I assure you, I'm not drunk."

The captain frowned. "Do you have any identification?"

"You bet I do. Here's my driver's license from the

state of Texas. Photo ID. And here's the rental agreement for the boat."

The captain perused the agreement. "This is one of François's boats. Did you rent it from him?"

"If that's his name, yes, I did."

"And he let you take it out alone?"

"He charged me enough for it."

"What security did he ask for?"

"He has my Platinum card and my passport. He knows he'll get his boat back."

"Were you planning on staying out here long?"

"Not anymore, I'm not. No offense, but you guys kind of took the joy out of it."

"Just doing our job."

"Of course."

The police asked him a few more questions and let him go. Teddy knew they would. If they declared him drunk and unfit to pilot a boat, they would have to tow it in, and they didn't want to do that.

As soon as the police were gone, Teddy packed up his gear to go. He cleaned up the beer cans and stowed his equipment. Without Maitland, the fishing gear fit in the duffel bag.

Teddy packed up the fishing pole. He got a surprise when he pulled in the line.

There was a fish on it.

57.

TEDDY PULLED THE cabin cruiser up to the dock. The man from the boat rental company was surprised to see him.

"Quitting so soon?"

"It gets boring after a while," Teddy said.

"What happened to your coolers?"

"I filled them with fish and dropped them off at the market."

"Yeah, sure."

Teddy grinned. "All right, I filled them with beer and dropped them off at a beach party."

"That I can believe."

Teddy got in the car and drove back to the hotel. It was nice handing it off to the valet without having to worry if he'd look in the trunk.

Teddy went into the lobby and used one of the hotel's computers to send an encrypted e-mail to Warplord924: Any news?

As he expected, Kevin was online. The answer came back almost immediately: Call me.

Teddy sighed. He logged off the computer, went back to his room, and called on a burner phone.

Kevin answered right away. "Is it you?"

"It's me. What's up? Don't tell me you were wrong about 'c).'"

"No, that was right. It's just more than you asked for."

"Oh?"

"You wanted one hit in the last few days. The name in question had almost a hundred."

"Really?"

"Yes. And I was able to trace them, too. Most of the searches originated in Syria. Does that upset your theory?"

"Not at all. You say 'most of the searches'?"

"Yeah. There were a couple from Paris. Does that make sense?"

"Yes, it does. Okay, good work."

"Is there anything else you need?"

"No, but check out the names now and then. See if anything else comes through."

"You think it will?"

"No."

Teddy hung up and assessed the situation. Kevin's news just confirmed that Workman was the man. The searches originating in Syria made perfect sense.

Teddy trashed the cell phone and took out another. He was going through them like water.

He called Jacques in Paris. "Do you know who this is?"

"Yes, I do. I didn't expect to hear from you."

"You're not. You haven't heard from me since I left."

"Of course. What do you need?"

"The reservations at l'Arrington. Could you look up the Syrian delegation for me?"

"Yes. Let me see. Syrians, party of five. Fahd, Syrian strongman, suspected arms dealer; Aziz, his personal bodyguard; and three scientists: two zoologists and one microbiologist. No, wait. I have a late cancellation. Make that two scientists."

"It wasn't the microbiologist who canceled, was it?"

"No. One of the zoologists."

"Do you have their names?"

"The zoologist is Dr. Chaim. The microbiologist is Dr. Badim."

"And when are they checking in?"

"Let's see. Actually, tonight."

"Good work. Remember, you didn't hear from me. I'll call you if I need you."

Teddy went down to the lobby and did a global search for the names Jacques had given him.

There was a lot about Fahd, none of it good. He was a strongman more feared than respected. What made him dangerous was his unpredictability. He was ostensibly in charge of terrorist activities, but it was not clear to whom he reported. Everyone reported to him, however. He was ruthless, cunning, and ambitious, a person to avoid. In every picture his eyes were hard. His face could be described as severe. He was unmarried, but known to enjoy the company of women.

Aziz had only one name, but that name was notorious. He was described as everything from Fahd's assistant to his bodyguard. The descriptions stopped just short of calling him Fahd's assassin.

There were no pictures of Aziz, but Teddy had a pretty good idea of who he was.

There was nothing about the zoology professor except his education and teaching position.

There was more on the microbiologist. He had his doctorate. His thesis was on infectious diseases.

TEDDY PUT ON a bathing suit and went down to the beach. He got a towel and a beach chair and an umbrella. He took off his shirt, kicked off his flip-flops, and waded into the sea.

It was the first time he'd been swimming since Lance had interrupted his rehab regimen. He wasn't really swimming now, mostly just bobbing up and down and making sure his head didn't go under. Teddy had removed his Stetson, but he was still made up like Floyd Maitland. It would be embarrassing if his moustache fell off.

After a nice dip, Teddy went back to the room, dried off, and put on the terry-cloth bathrobe the hotel provided.

Maitland had an iPad in his briefcase. Teddy switched it on and scrolled through the man's e-mails to see if there was anything useful. He found a few dealing with the convention, but nothing particularly helpful. Teddy hadn't really expected to find an e-mail with the subject line "Hunt an Endangered Species." Still, there was nothing to indicate that Floyd Maitland's interest in rare animals was in any way out of the ordinary.

Teddy googled Floyd Maitland to see if he could come up with anything that would help with his impersonation of the man. If he met someone Maitland knew well, nothing would help, but barring that, any little thing might sell the facade.

His search was fruitless. Jacques had done a good job. Teddy didn't find anything he didn't already know.

Teddy switched his search to images. In all the pictures there were certain constants. Maitland always wore his Stetson hat. And he always wore his cowboy boots. And he always wore a broad leather belt with an ornate buckle. Teddy wished Maitland's belt fit him, but the one he had bought would be close enough.

Teddy noticed one other thing.

In almost all of the photos Maitland also wore a gun belt and holster, with what appeared to be a .45-caliber Colt revolver. He wasn't wearing it at what appeared to be a banquet, but otherwise it was always there.

Teddy had searched Maitland's room pretty thoroughly, and could have sworn no such gun was in it, but he searched it again. It was easier this time, since he knew what he was looking for. Starting with the premise of where a .45-caliber Colt revolver might hide, there were not a lot of options. It did not take long for Teddy to satisfy himself the gun was not there.

Teddy couldn't imagine the man traveling without it, despite the trouble it would take to smuggle it into France.

Teddy got dressed, put on his Stetson hat, and went down to the front desk. "Excuse me. Floyd Maitland. I'm in room four three two."

"Yes. Mr. Maitland."

"Help me out, willya, pardner?" Teddy shook his head ruefully. "I am juggling so many things I just can't keep track of what I'm doing. Did I leave anything in the hotel safe, or was that at the last hotel?"

"Let me check." The clerk looked it up. "Yes, Mr. Maitland. You left a box to be placed in the hotel safe. It's there now."

"Well, that's a relief. Could I have it, please? I'm checking out tomorrow. It would be just like me to forget it."

"Of course, Mr. Maitland. You understand the safe is locked. I will have to get the manager to open it."

"I'd be worried if you didn't," Teddy said.

Fifteen minutes later the desk clerk presented Teddy with the box. Teddy took it up to Maitland's room and opened it. Inside was exactly what he expected: a gun belt and holster with a .45-caliber Colt revolver. The revolver was empty, but the loops in the gun belt all held bullets—and there was a box of ammunition. Teddy took the revolver, flipped the cylinder out, spun it, and flipped it closed again.

Teddy put the gun belt on, and slipped the .45 into the holster.

He looked good in it.

58.

TEDDY FLEW BACK to Paris the next day. He was alert leaving baggage claim, in case Maitland had arranged for someone to meet the plane. He hadn't. Teddy got a cab, took it to l'Arrington, and checked in at the front desk.

"Floyd Maitland. I have a reservation."

"Ah. Yes, Monsieur Maitland. You are in the mini-suite. Six nineteen."

"'Mini-suite'!" Teddy said. "Son, I'm from Texas. There ain't nothing *mini* about me. You must be mistaken."

The clerk blinked and adjusted to the situation. The guest, however unreasonable, was always right. "But of course, monsieur. We have a standard suite for you, just as you requested. You are in fourteen oh five."

"That's more like it, then," Teddy said. He had a feeling suite 1405 was exactly the same as suite 619.

"Are you here for the convention, monsieur?"

"That's right."

"Registration for the convention is on the mezzanine level."

"'Registration'? I'm registered."

"But of course. Registration is where you check in. You will be given a program and schedule and your name tag."

"Fine," Teddy said. "Now then, I have some valuables I would like to store in the hotel safe. Do I give them to you?"

"Absolutely. There is a safe in your suite, but anything too large for it, we would be happy to keep for you. Now, if I could have your credit card and photo ID."

The desk clerk ran Teddy's credit card, and then passed it and the ID back. "Now, if you would just sign here."

Teddy had practiced signing Maitland's signature on the plane. He dashed off a pretty convincing facsimile.

The desk clerk couldn't have cared less. He was already clapping his hands for a bellboy. "Take monsieur to fourteen oh five."

As he stepped into the elevator, Teddy smiled at how easy it was to impersonate a wealthy Texan. Loud and brash seemed to do the trick.

Teddy followed the bellboy to a suite that was much more luxurious than he needed. It even had a hot tub. He unpacked, and then took the box containing Maitland's gun belt down to the front desk. The clerk assured him that whatever was in the box would be safely locked away.

Teddy went up to the mezzanine level where he found a long table with three members of the convention staff sitting behind it. On the table in front of them were signs: A—G, H—O, and P—Z. it took Teddy a moment to recall his name was Maitland and he should be in the H—O line.

"Hi," he said. "Floyd Maitland. I'm registered with the convention."

The staff woman waiting on him riffled through the file cards in a little box and came up with a printed name tag. "Here you go. Floyd Maitland. Oh! You have a star on your name tag." She held it up and showed it to him. The name tag had the conference logo, which was a baby panda, and the name FLOYD MAITLAND in large letters. Under the name, in smaller bold type, it read: USA. In the bottom right corner there was a gold star printed on the name tag.

"And what's that mean, ma'am?" Teddy said.

The woman positively beamed. "It signifies your registration for the special panel, the one by invitation only."

"Ahh yes, of course."

"I've been handing out the name tags and there weren't that many stars. You must be very important!"

"Just know the right people, I guess," Teddy said. He was grateful for the woman's enthusiasm—now he knew that anyone else with a star on their name tag would also be attending the mysterious panel.

The woman grabbed one of the canvas bags behind her and set it on the table. "Inside you will find your name tag holder, program, and schedule with the full description of the panels, so you can choose which ones you want to go to. And there's a map of the hotel, showing where the panel rooms are. There are also some promotional materials, including some books authored by fellow attendees. It's a lot to carry around. You'll probably want to stash it in your room before you start exploring."

"And the panels start tomorrow?"

"That's right. There's an opening reception tonight at six in the grand ballroom. The only event going on now is the animal exhibit."

"'Animal exhibit'?"

"Oh, yes. A wide variety of small animals is on display in the convention center. But you'll probably want to steer clear."

"Oh? Why?"

She smiled. "It's a zoo."

59.

I T WAS A ZOO in more ways than one. The convention hall was filled with animals and their handlers, and in addition to the hotel guests, the organizers had sold day passes to the public as part of their conservation fundraising. The convention floor was mobbed with families with children pressing forward to see the creatures.

Ironically, some of the less rare species grabbed the most attention. Leopard cubs, lion cubs, indeed anything with cub, was immensely popular, and understandably so. They were incredibly cute.

Teddy made a circuit of the floor, looking for fellow conventioneers, identified by the cloth name tag pouches worn around the neck. There weren't many yet.

Teddy gave up on the convention area and decided to look in the bar. It was jammed. Evidently, everyone else had had the same idea. Patrons were lined up three deep the whole length of the bar trying to order drinks.

The Syrian contingent might have been there, but there was no way to tell. Teddy decided to wait for the opening ceremony. It would be easy to spot his quarry then. All he had to do was meet them.

It wouldn't be easy. Friendly and gregarious was unlikely to be their manner. Teddy expected the Syrians to keep to themselves, and resist any intrusion on their privacy. Not that that would stop him. Teddy was lucky to have chosen a loud, flamboyant persona. Missing social cues and being aggressively friendly was right in character. The fact that they all had stars on their name tags could be seized upon as a momentous occurrence, rather than just noted in passing.

Toward that end, Teddy figured it would be good if the Syrians noticed him before he made his approach. He just had to make sure that happened.

Teddy went back to the front desk.

"Excuse me. Floyd Maitland. I just checked in. I left a box in the hotel safe."

"Yes, sir."

"Could I get it, please?"

60.

T HE GRAND BALLROOM was set up for the opening ceremony. There were cash bars in all four corners, with free wine and soft drinks at tables in between. There was a buffet table down the middle, which proved to have an assortment of hors d'oeuvres.

The ballroom was crowded, but not nearly so much as the convention hall zoo. The convention itself was not a family affair. The plight of endangered species was a serious business that drew the attention of the most noted scientists and conservationists from around the world.

Teddy was decked out for the opening ceremony in his cowboy boots, Stetson hat, blue jeans, and leather jacket.

He also wore his six-shooter, which he twirled occasionally. He was quite good at it. He'd practiced up in his room, but it didn't take much. Teddy had played cowboys as a stuntman. He could draw the gun, twirl it, and stick it back in the holster in one fluid motion, without ever taking his eyes off the man he was looking at.

Teddy got himself bourbon on the rocks. He elbowed his way through the crowd, holding his drink aloft, and looking for the Syrians.

He spotted Aziz first. The little hit man had just gotten a drink at the cash bar. It was clear, probably vodka. He tossed it off, set the glass down, and marched back to the others.

Teddy took a moment to size up the group. Fahd was frightening. He was a remorseless, take-no-prisoners type, every bit as deadly as Aziz. But while the little hit man would kill, Fahd would order it done.

Teddy had no problem sorting out the scientists. The severe, humorless one who looked like he belonged behind a Bunsen burner would be the microbiologist. The fidgety, nervous one who looked eager to please would be the zoologist. Teddy wondered if the man was just shy in social situations, or if his anxiety had anything to do with the fact that there had originally been *two* Syrian zoologists scheduled to attend and, the unsettling thought, maybe *they* were an endangered species.

Teddy finished off his drink. He bellied up to the bar. "Hey, barkeep! Barkeep! Another bourbon on the rocks!" When the bartender handed it to him, Teddy handed it back. "No! Make it a double!" he cried, pushing his hat brim back with the barrel of his Colt forty-five.

The bartender's eyes widened. "I don't believe you're allowed to have that in here."

"Nonsense," Teddy said. "Show me the rule. If you can't show me the rule, I don't have to do it." He slapped money down on the bar, said "Keep it," and grabbed his drink. "See? I'm a sport. Only got a single, and I paid you for a double. How do you like that?"

As he turned away from the table, out of the corner of

his eye Teddy could see the bartender beckon one of the hotel staff over.

Teddy waved his drink with one hand and his Stetson with the other. He clapped his hat back on his head, drew his gun, twirled it, and returned it to the holster with a flourish. He careened into the middle of the floor, stopped, and took a huge pull of his drink. He drew his gun and twirled it again.

Many of the other guests were edging away from him, and men in hotel staff uniforms were weaving their way through the crowd.

A man who appeared to be with hotel security came walking up. "Excuse me," he said, quietly. "If monsieur would please come with me."

"No, I won't come with you," Teddy said loudly. "I paid a lot to be at this convention, and I got a right to be here."

"I need to talk to you."

"If you want to talk to me, do it after the reception."

"I'm sorry, monsieur, but you cannot bring a gun into the royal ballroom. It is against the law."

"Prove it," Teddy said.

The security guard was taken aback. The man with him, probably a desk clerk, said in a conciliatory manner, "Monsieur, we would prefer not to involve the authorities. If you would care to leave your gun at the front desk, we would be glad to hold it for you, but you cannot have it here."

"In my country we have second amendment rights," Teddy said.

"In your country, I would not bother you. In my country, I must hold your gun."

"All right," Teddy said. "But you owe me a drink. Tell him to give me a drink on the house."

The staffman nodded to the bartender.

"Bourbon," Teddy said. He took off his gun belt, handed it over, and headed for the bar. He didn't need the gun belt anymore. It had served its purpose.

Everyone knew who he was.

61.

A PROFESSORIAL-LOOKING GENTLEMAN in a tweed jacket tapped on the microphone. "Good evening, ladies and gentlemen, I am Lucius Camus, and I am delighted to be hosting the third annual Endangered Species Preservation Conference."

There was a round of applause.

"We want you to know how much we value your support for this worthy cause. In addition to the pledge drives, raffle tickets, and charity auctions, nothing beats a cash donation. And nothing makes you feel better than to know you are contributing to the preservation of these endangered species.

"But you are here to enjoy yourselves, as I am sure you will. We have triple-track programming scheduled. We're sorry you won't be able to attend all the panels, but you will always have three excellent options to choose from. Afterward, you can exchange ideas with someone who saw one of the others. And I happen to know some of our lecturers, if you buy them a drink in the bar, they will never stop talking."

This sally was met with appreciative laughter.

"Panels will begin tomorrow morning at nine. All panels are open to everyone, except for those few panels designated by a star. Only guests with stars on their name tags will be admitted to those panels. Please don't feel discriminated against. It's because they paid extra."

Lucius gestured to the man standing next to him. "And now, it is my great pleasure to introduce Monsieur René Darjon, our benefactor, who has generously underwritten the conference for the third year running. Without his help, none of this would have been possible. Ladies and gentlemen, Monsieur René Darjon!"

René Darjon stepped to the microphone. He was a strikingly handsome man, with silver sideburns and a trim moustache. In a custom-tailored navy-blue suit, he looked like he would be equally comfortable spearheading a multimillion-dollar business deal or escorting a movie star to a Hollywood film awards. He was the type of man who was catnip to the ladies, and knew it.

René Darjon dismissed the applause as unnecessary; though Teddy had a feeling he'd have been miffed if he didn't get it. His smile was benevolent, if a trifle condescending.

"My friends. I cannot thank you enough for showing up to support this worthy cause. I am doing everything I can to aid these endangered species, but I cannot do it alone. Now, more than ever, we need your support. Listen to what the panelists have to say, and let your hearts unlock your checkbooks. This is our third annual conference. Let's make it the best one ever."

As René Darjon stepped away from the microphone,

a stunning brunette in an evening dress slipped her arm through his and draped herself on his shoulder. He put his arm around her, and held her to him. She smiled up at him affectionately.

It was Kristin.

RENÉ DARJON LEFT with Kristin shortly after he spoke. Teddy didn't try to follow. He didn't want to hover over her, and he had other fish to fry. Instead, he detoured back to his room, took out a fresh burner phone, and called Jacques.

"You know who this is?"

"Glad you called. We've got trouble."

"Oh?"

"Workman's gone dark."

"Oh?"

"At first I thought he was just undercover, but no one knows where he is. There are rumors bouncing around. He defected. He was abducted. He was a mole to begin with. Or that he's dead."

"What's the general consensus?"

"There is none, just a lot of conflicting opinions."

"What does Norton think?"

"He's too cool to let on."

"Is anything being done to locate him?"

"I'm out of that loop. The fact that he's missing is gossip. What's being done about it is intel."

"Right."

"What's your theory?"

"I don't have one."

"So what do you want me to do?"

"Let me know if they find him."

"Will do. So, why'd you call?"

"Two things. What have you got on René Darjon?"

"The Silver Fox?"

"I beg your pardon?"

"That's what they call him. The Silver Fox. What about him?"

"He's underwriting the convention. Is he a great philanthropist?"

"Not that I know of. He never puts money into anything that doesn't turn a profit. He's a ruthless corporate CEO who built his empire through hostile takeovers and leveraged buyouts. Contributing to a cause is completely out of character."

"Is that right?"

"Oh, yes. But taking the credit for it isn't. He's the type who's happy accepting a humanitarian award on TV at the same time he's purchasing cheap real estate and evicting the tenants to put up a factory."

"You didn't know he was at the conference?"

"I don't know anything about the conference except who has hotel reservations for it. René Darjon lives in Paris. He maintains a hotel room full time for his assignations, but it's not at l'Arrington."

"Nice guy. And you don't know what his angle here is?"

"Like I say, I didn't even know he was there."

"What about the Agency?"

"What about it?"

"As far as you know, they haven't taken any interest in the convention?"

"Not at all. If any agents have taken an interest, they're pursuing it outside official channels. Not totally atypical for early reconnaissance, if the agent just has a hunch but nothing to back it up yet," Jacques said. "But once they check in, they have to report to the chief and get his go-ahead on an official mission."

"Interesting."

"Why is that interesting?"

Teddy laughed. "It's the type of thing people say when they don't understand what's going on."

Teddy hung up the phone. He wasn't happy. Kristin's presence at the conference wasn't good. From what he'd learned of her, she fancied herself a female James Bond. Going off on her own and failing to report in to Norton was her standard MO.

Teddy wondered if Kristin's investigation was due to Workman's disappearance. As far as she was concerned, he was a fellow agent, not a mole. She must have backtracked what he was working on and found a link to the Syrians, not realizing he was actually in their pocket. She'd follow his lead on the conference, and want to finish up what Workman had started. The fact that he was missing and presumed dead wouldn't faze her. To her, it would be an incentive. To avenge a fellow agent. She'd want to check out the conference and see what the Syrians were up to. She couldn't come at them directly, and risk winding up like Workman, but she needed an overview of what was going on. The answer was René Darjon, the playboy entrepreneur who was financing the convention. Making a play for him was just the type of flamboyant gesture she'd be apt to try. On his arm, she'd have access to everything. And he'd be eager to show off. Through him, she could get inside information on the Syrians. Her only problem was, she couldn't approach them directly.

Teddy could.

62.

TEDDY WENT BACK to the barroom, grabbed a glass of bourbon, and barged up to the Syrians. "Hey, star buddies!" he said, pointing at the stars on the name tags. "I heard what that guy said. We're the chosen ones. Can you say that? Is that a religion thing, or something? We can go to the panel and they can't, right, buddy?"

Fahd turned up his nose. "It is just another panel. For which we happen to have admission." He spoke swiftly and quietly, an obvious effort to quiet down the brash Texan.

"Of course, of course," Teddy said. "I don't mean to be loud, I just am. We do things big in Texas. Not a quiet state. But look what happened here. Took my gun. Did you see that? Actually took my gun. I feel naked without it."

Fahd said nothing and tried to ignore him.

"I'm a big-game hunter," Teddy persisted. "Do you hunt?" He looked at Aziz. "I bet he does."

Aziz's expression did not change. Clearly he hadn't recognized Teddy.

Teddy turned back to Fahd. "Floyd Maitland. Pleased to meet you."

Fahd ignored the extended hand. "Mr. Maitland, the instructions regarding the small panel were quite specific, and chief among them is the discretion of the attendees. I suggest you read them over." Fahd turned away and began to gather his group, but Teddy was not deterred. He turned to the two scientists, Dr. Chaim and Dr. Badim according to Jacques's notes. "You guys read 'em?"

The scientists looked at each other.

"Hey," Teddy said. "This is a party. Have a drink. Loosen up."

The zoologist had a drink. That would be Dr. Chaim. He held it up, as if for show-and-tell.

Teddy shook his head. "You guys look like you're on your way to the gallows. Hey, let me buy you a round."

"That is not necessary," Fahd said.

"Of course it isn't necessary. It's a gesture of goodwill." Teddy turned to Dr. Badim. "You there. Drink up, drink up. What are you going to do, nurse one drink all evening? This is a party. Drink up, I'll get you another. And you there," he said to Dr. Chaim. "What are you having?"

Dr. Chaim looked guilty, as if he'd been caught with it. "A Manhattan."

Teddy burst out laughing. "'A Manhattan'? How about that. You're drinking our drinks, I'd watch this one. He might just defect."

Fahd did not find that funny. Teddy hadn't expected him to. Goading the strongman was part of his game. It was also fun.

"So what will *you* have?" Teddy asked Fahd.

"I'm not drinking."

"No, no, no, no, no. You've gotta have something. You don't have to have some candy-ass American drink, but something. What will it be?"

Fahd realized the man wouldn't give up until he answered. "Vodka."

"On the rocks?"

"No."

"And you?" Teddy said to Aziz.

"He will have vodka."

"Did you hear that?" Teddy said. "*You* will have vodka."

Teddy plowed his way to the bar, pulling out money as he went. "Lotta drinks," he announced. "Three shots of vodka, a Manhattan, and a bourbon on the rocks." He waved a hundred-dollar bill at the bartender. "Can you take it out of this?"

"But of course."

"Good. Put 'em on a tray, and you can keep whatever's left."

All thoughts of Teddy being a nuisance were forgotten. The bartender was all too happy to fill the order.

Teddy took the tray back to the Syrian contingent.

"Here you go. Bottoms up. That's what we say in my country. It means drink the damn thing, don't just hold it. See? Drinking turns the bottom of the glass up." Teddy handed the Manhattan to Dr. Chaim. "Oh. You got a straw." He shrugged. "'Bottoms up' doesn't work with straws."

Fahd was clearly planning his group's exit.

Teddy waved his arms, calling everyone into a huddle.

"Come here. Come here. Look. About the panel. I'm not going to say anything. I'm going to be quiet like a mouse. But it meets every day, right? And the first session is tomorrow afternoon?"

Teddy included the two scientists. "You boys will be going to that?"

Dr. Badim said nothing, but Dr. Chaim, eager to please, said, "Yes. And there is an introductory meeting for our panel tonight at nine."

The look Fahd gave Dr. Chaim was pure venom.

63.

TEDDY TONED IT down for the panel. He'd created enough of an impression for the Syrians, and didn't need to draw any further attention.

The panel was, as Teddy had expected, in the room Marcel DuBois had shown him, the one with the single solid door.

There were two men at the door checking names. It was not enough to show your name tag with the star, you also had to show a photo ID to prove that you were the person named on it, and not someone who just happened to get hold of the name tag. The men were passing themselves off as convention staff, but Teddy recognized them for what they really were: muscle.

Teddy saw the Syrian party was already seated in the front row, and he took a seat in the second row at the opposite end of the room.

More panel goers drifted in. They filled the first three rows. Nobody sat behind Teddy in his cowboy hat.

The meeting included gentlemen of all nationalities. Many had zoologists in tow.

When everyone had been seated and the doors had

been closed and locked, Fernand Guillaume, a dapper Frenchman with the air of an auctioneer, took the lectern. He glanced around the room and smiled. "My friends. Have any of you been to Las Vegas? There is a saying, 'What happens in Vegas, stays in Vegas.' The same is true of this panel. Since you are here, you already know that. But I cannot emphasize it enough. Anybody found to have loose lips will be banned from any future opportunities of this kind."

No one took exception to the remark. It was greeted with nods of approval.

"Now then. Down to business. This panel is entitled Rarest of the Rare. That is absolutely true. Our presenters will be showing you some of the rarest animals in the world. Many are on the endangered species list. Some will be there soon. There is one unifying factor. It is illegal to hunt these animals. A violation of this law carries a stiff sentence.

"In the privacy of this room, we acknowledge the distinction between laws of man and of nature. We speak freely behind locked doors. And we never speak freely outside them. Only in this room may your business be conducted.

"We are divided into two groups. The buyers and the sellers. You may sell the animals. You may buy the animals. No one is going to ask you what you wish to do with the animal you bought."

Though Teddy had anticipated the secret purpose of the mysterious and exclusive panel, he was still jolted to hear the truth of it. An illicit marketplace of endangered animals, hiding in plain sight, right in the midst of a conference on conservation.

"Some animals will be presented on the panel. Some can be seen on exhibit in the convention center. The larger animals will be shown in photos and on videotape, and our organization has verified the existence and advertised condition of those creatures.

"The auction will begin tomorrow, so for now I hope only to whet your appetite."

He stepped aside and gestured to the screen behind him. A video montage showed some of the animals in question. A snow leopard, a sea otter, lemurs, and a fierce-looking, rodent-like creature that apparently was a Tasmanian devil. A polar bear that looked scrawny. Teddy wondered if that was part of the allure, shooting a truly endangered, sick animal.

The black rhino looked positively magnificent. When it appeared on screen, it was as if the room took a collective breath. Teddy glimpsed over at the Syrians to gauge their reaction, but Fahd and Aziz wore carefully blank faces.

One of the animals on offer was of particular interest to them, though which was still unclear to Teddy. The bigger question was: What did Fahd want with an endangered animal in the first place?

64.

TEDDY NOTICED ONE of the German contingent seated at the bar. He squeezed in next to the German and ordered a bourbon on the rocks. When it came he raised it, took a sip, and made it seem as if he had noticed the German for the first time.

The German's name was Hans. He had a star on his name tag. Teddy pointed to it. "You were at the panel."

"Da."

"You speak English?"

Hans waggled his hand. The German had a blond crew cut, broad shoulders, and a solid build. He could have passed for a gym coach.

Or a hunter.

Teddy lowered his voice. "Do you shoot?"

Hans shrugged, helplessly.

Teddy mimed raising a rifle.

Hans pushed his arms down. He lowered his voice. "You do not do that here."

Teddy grinned. "I thought you knew a little English. Hey, barkeep. Give my friend a beer."

The bartender lined another beer up behind the one Hans was drinking.

Teddy lowered his voice. "No more gestures. I think we understand each other. We're here because we like animals. Now, I like a Siberian tiger myself."

Hans frowned. "You use many words."

"Sorry," Teddy said. "What animal do you like?"

The German's eyes gleamed. "Black rhino."

"Yes," Teddy said. "That would be something. I've never even seen a black rhino."

Another German appeared behind Hans. His name was Fritz. He was clearly cut from the same mold as Hans, though he appeared to be in charge. He launched into a torrent of German.

Teddy couldn't catch every word, but he knew enough German to catch the gist of what Fritz was saying. He was reminding Hans not to be indiscreet.

Teddy excused himself, giving Hans a hearty slap on the shoulder as he left. He wandered around the bar, striking up conversations with any panelists he could.

It wasn't easy.

The Chinese contingent kept to themselves. The Russians were rowdy, throwing back shots of vodka and talking loudly in Russian, but it seemed to be mostly about World Cup soccer and the attributes of the waitress. And the Palestinians did not seem to be present. Still, Teddy managed to collect a good deal of information.

A random sampling of the people in the bar confirmed his theory.

The groups with scientists couldn't have cared less about the black rhino. Their objectives remained opaque to him.

The groups with hunters wanted to kill it.

Not if he could help it.

65.

MILLIE MET LANCE in front of the lion cage.

"The National Zoo?" Lance said irritably.

"Our friend thought it would be fitting."

"This is not a joke, Millie. This is serious business."

"I will pass the sentiment along, but do you expect our friend to be chastened by it?"

"You're pretty sassy lately."

"Sorry. I'm trying to give you the flavor of the communication. Our friend's attitude tends to seep through."

"So, what's the news? What's he up to?"

"He's making progress. He expects to uncover the mole, but not by infiltrating the embassy as you'd intended. It's essential that everyone think he's gone home. Then they'll let down their guard."

"I know his theory. You told me that last time. I didn't like it then, and I don't like it now. Why am I here?"

"He needs petty cash money. He needs you to wire it to a bank in Paris. I have the account number."

"You dragged me out here for petty cash?"

"That's right."

"For God's sake, couldn't you advance it yourself?"

"I'm afraid not. He needs a half million euros right away, no questions asked, no strings attached. It's the only way under which the operation can continue. If he can't get it, he's coming home."

"He's *extorting* me?"

"He said you'd use that word."

"He wants a half million euros and he won't say why?"

"Actually, he did. He needs to buy something in order to keep up his cover."

"He needs to buy something? For a half million euros? What does he need to buy?"

"A black rhino."

Lance's mouth fell open. "He wants to buy a black rhino?"

"Yes."

"That's why he had us meet in the zoo?"

"He said you'd say that, too. He could practically have this conversation without you."

"Okay. Why does he want to buy a black rhino? What's he going to do with it?"

"Shoot it."

66.

TEDDY GOT UP the next morning and checked his e-mail. Sure enough, there was an encrypted e-mail from Millie. Money being transferred. Should be in by this morning.

He showered, dressed in another Floyd Maitland getup, and made his way down to the hotel restaurant for breakfast. Teddy spotted one of the Palestinians in the lobby. There were four of them, according to Jacques, two of them scientists. But this man had a military bearing.

He also had a hostile air. Teddy would have given him a wide berth, but the man made a point of walking right up to him.

Omar, according to his name tag, said, "Do I know you?" Somehow he made it sound like an accusation.

Teddy grinned. "Well now, I don't believe we've met. Unless it was sometime when I'd had a few. Floyd Maitland. Pleased to meet you."

Omar made no move to take his outstretched hand. His eyes ran over Teddy's face, as if memorizing every detail. "Is that so?" he said, coldly. Then he turned and walked away.

Teddy snapped a picture of Omar with his cell phone. He would have texted it to Jacques, to run through face recognition, but he was out of burner phones, and he couldn't risk using his own.

Teddy went back to the lobby computer. He uploaded the photo from his phone, and sent Kevin an encrypted e-mail. Kevin. Run the attached photo through face recognition. Yes, I know you don't have access to the CIA database, but do it anyway. He's going by the name of Omar, but it may be an alias. Get back to me as fast as you can. Your answer will tell me what I have to do.

The last part wasn't entirely true. Teddy knew what he had to do, regardless of Kevin's answer. He had to get some more burner phones and pick up a half million euros.

Up to now Teddy had trusted Maitland's room safe for a few choice possessions. Omar's malevolent presence made that no longer tenable. Teddy opened the safe and took out his handgun, his cash supply, and his travel equipment bag, with a few special items he'd held out from the larger equipment bag locked in the hotel safe at the St. Pierre.

Teddy spent a few minutes booby-trapping the room so that he would know if Omar had been there. Then he took off his Floyd Maitland outfit, and dressed up as Devon Billingham. He touched up his face to make sure it matched the passport photo, and took a cab to the Hôtel St. Pierre.

He walked up to the front desk and said, "Hi, Devon Billingham. Are there any messages for me?"

The desk clerk checked. "Ah, Monsieur Billingham. There are no messages, but your room has not been used for several days."

"Yes, I said that might happen. That's why I paid for the week in advance. I had to make some side trips. But I'm here now and would like to retrieve a trunk that was stored for me in the hotel safe." Teddy slipped the desk clerk a bill. "Could you expedite that for me, please?"

"Would you like the trunk brought to your room?"

"Yes. How soon will that be done?"

"Right away."

Teddy went up to his room. It didn't look lived in. The only sign of occupancy were the toiletries in the bathroom.

He called the bank. "This is Devon Billingham. I'm awaiting a transfer of funds. Can you tell me if it's been processed yet? I want to come down to the bank and complete the transaction. Yes, I'll hold."

There was a knock on the door. It was the bellboy with the trunk. He tipped the bellboy and said into the phone, "Really? Good. I'll be right down."

Teddy unlocked the trunk, took out three more burner phones, and locked it up again. When he left he would leave it at the front desk to be returned to the safe. He would have loved to have transferred it to l'Arrington, but he didn't want to deal with having two packages in their safe. Plus, the less overlap of identities the better, even in something so trivial. In Teddy's experience, one never knew who might be taking an interest.

Teddy messed up the bedsheets—so the chambermaid would stop worrying about it—and went down to the bank.

ONCE THE BANKERS realized who Teddy was, he was treated like a king. A sudden infusion of a half million euros into his bank account had earned him instant respect. Assistant managers were falling all over each other, asking how they might assist him.

His answer did not please them. They disappeared into the inner office with the news. Moments later, the bank manager himself came out. He surveilled Teddy critically, and frowned.

"You want a cashier's check for five hundred thousand euros?"

"I do."

"You are taking your money out of the bank?"

"Not all of my money. Just the most recent deposit."

"I don't understand."

"I want to transfer funds. I need a cashier's check to do it. I want your bank to provide it."

"You do not intend to keep the half million euros in our bank?"

"Not *that* half million."

"You intend to deposit another half million?"

"I might," Teddy said. "It depends on the service I receive here."

Five minutes later the head teller delivered a cashier's check for five hundred thousand euros. The bank manager presented it with a bit of a flourish.

Teddy inspected it, smiled, and slipped it into his jacket pocket.

The bank manager looked horrified. "You need to sign it."

"I signed for the check."

"You need to sign the *check*. If you don't sign the check, anyone can. It's as good as cash. Anyone can make it out to anyone they want, and sign their name. And then you would have no right to it."

"But I have the check."

"What if the check is stolen?"

"Do you expect the check to be stolen?"

"It's not what I expect. But it could happen."

"But no one knows I have it. Unless your bank told someone. Is your bank in the habit of advertising the business of its depositors?"

While the bank manager struggled to think of a response, Teddy shook his hand, turned, and walked out.

TEDDY WENT BACK to the St. Pierre. He logged on to a computer in the lobby and sent an encrypted e-mail to Kevin. The answer came back almost immediately. Kevin had obviously composed it already, and was just waiting for a prompt. Omar's full name was Omar Khalidi. He was rumored to have taken part in death squads, often as leader. His ruthlessness was legendary.

Teddy had never encountered him under that name or any other. But the man clearly had acted as if he knew him. It might have been merely his style of intimidation; still, Teddy wondered why he bothered. Perhaps Floyd Maitland's ugly-American act had just rubbed him the wrong way.

Whatever the reason, Teddy would have to be on his guard.

67.

TEDDY TOOK A cab back to l'Arrington. He was still dressed as Devon Billingham, but that didn't matter. In the crowd of the convention, no one would notice him at all, at least not in the common areas. He just couldn't let anyone see Devon Billingham entering Maitland's room with a hotel key card.

He was in luck. Two people got on the elevator, but neither pushed his floor. He got out of the elevator alone, walked down to Maitland's room, and went in.

A man was sitting there.

It was Omar.

He was holding a gun.

Omar's eyes were hard, triumphant. "Not so smart as you think, are you?"

"Clearly not."

"You thought no one would see past that fake moustache and stupid cowboy hat. But I do. You are not Floyd Maitland."

Teddy shrugged. "It was a calculated risk."

"Unfortunately for you, I've had dealings with Maitland.

He was an annoying man but a good businessman, sold us AK-47s."

"I hope you got a good deal."

Omar gestured with the gun. "With one hand, reach down and pull your jacket open so I can see your gun."

Teddy did as he was told. The shoulder holster hung just where Omar said it would.

"Take the gun out with two fingers and set it on the floor. Slowly. That's it. Now stand up and raise your hands again. Don't make any sudden moves. You're mine. I could have shot you. I still can. But I want to know who you are and what you're doing. Are you with the CIA?"

"I am not with the CIA."

"Who are you with?"

Teddy just smiled.

Omar scowled. "You have no bargaining power. You talk or you die."

"I will talk. Just ask me something I know."

"You don't know who you're with?"

"I don't know what the sides are. I don't know what the game is. So far, all I know is several people want to kill a black rhino. Why, I have no idea."

"For sport."

"So they say. But you don't want to kill it. Why not?"

"It does not amuse me."

"I doubt if this operation was organized for your amusement. Why was it organized, I wonder?"

Omar said nothing. He rubbed his left eye.

Teddy relaxed slightly.

Omar frowned. "You look too calm. Why aren't you frightened?"

"They teach us not to show fear. It's one of the first classes at Langley."

Omar scowled.

"That gun must be heavy with the silencer," Teddy said. "Why don't you put it down?"

"Last chance," Omar snarled. "You want to talk, or should I shoot you right now?"

"Hmm. Tough choice. They're always mad at you when you talk. When you're shot, you get a lot of sympathy."

"Stop talking nonsense!"

"Did you open my hotel safe?" Teddy said gently.

The change of subject was too much for Omar. He blinked stupidly. "What?"

"My hotel safe. Did you open it?"

"There was nothing in it."

"But you opened it. Which hand did you use?"

"Why?"

"You're right-handed, aren't you? You're holding the gun in your right hand. But some right-handed people use their left hand on a combination lock. Is that what you did?"

"Why are you saying this?"

"Just passing the time. Why exactly did you open the safe? What were you looking for?"

"Why are you being so strange?"

"You're very strong, aren't you? Were you ever captured? I bet you'd stand up well to interrogation. Strong man like you. And yet . . ." Teddy pointed. "I was right!

Your left eyelid's drooping. You *did* use your left hand on the safe."

The Palestinian blinked, no longer sure of himself. "What are you saying?"

"I figured you'd search my room and open my safe. You know, it's amazing that a small amount of serum can produce such a drastic result. Could you feel the pinprick on your finger? Obviously not, or you would not have been waiting so patiently for me to get home."

Omar shuddered. The gun he was holding wavered. He raised it at Teddy and attempted to pull the trigger. But his finger was putty.

"Can't hold a gun anymore, can you? It's all right, I'll help you." Teddy stepped up and took the gun from Omar's fingers. "Good thing you're sitting down or you'd be on the floor by now."

Teddy pulled open the door of the minibar and took out a small, clear bottle. "You want the antidote?" He popped open the bottle and poured it into a small glass. "You have maybe a minute before you won't be able to drink it anymore. You can take comfort in the fact that you were loyal and true in the face of death, or you can tell me why you're at the conference. You don't have time for a lengthy explanation, so just give me the gist." He held up the glass, tantalizingly. "Why are you here?"

Omar's face twisted. His mouth was distorted, making it impossible to tell if he was trying to talk or just writhing in agony.

His mouth formed a word. "Dog."

Teddy blinked. *Dog?*

Omar was now swaying. Teddy gripped his shoulders and shook him. "Did you say 'dog'?" he asked.

Omar nodded his head, sort of a lolling droop, but a clear affirmative.

"Good boy. Drink this." He held the glass to Omar's lips. Omar managed to choke it down. "And here's the rest of the antidote." Teddy took a hypodermic syringe out of his pocket. He rolled up Omar's sleeve, and injected it into his vein. Omar's body jerked violently. "Don't worry. That's perfectly natural."

The twitching subsided.

"Now, here's the bad news. That wasn't the antidote. The drink was vodka. The injection was pure alcohol. I need you to have enough in your system that no one questions an accident. That's right. You're going to have an accident. Just sit there. I'll take care of everything."

Teddy opened the hotel room door. Maitland's suite was on the interior court, where the hallway overlooked the lobby fourteen floors below. At the moment, the chambermaids were working in suites across the court, and there was no one in the hall. Teddy went back, lifted Omar to his feet, and walked him to the door. The man had no conscious thought remaining, just a few motor functions. Teddy propped him up, opened the door, and looked out. There was still no one there. Teddy pulled him out, leaned him on the rail, hoisted him up, and flipped him over.

Teddy didn't wait to see the result. He was back in Maitland's suite with the door locked before the body landed in the lobby.

68.

THE PANEL BEGAN on a somber note. Most of the attendees were in place and the door was locked when Fernand took the lectern. Conspicuous by his absence was one of the Palestine group.

"My friends. You all know we have lost one of our number. It is a tragedy, but it is also a caution. This is not the time or place to be indulging in weaknesses. If you have a problem with alcohol, with drugs, with sex, with gambling, you must control these urges."

Fernand gave them all a stern look. Then he smiled. "But now to the business at hand. This is what you have all been waiting for, a chance to own some of the rarest animals still living on the planet.

"And let us start off with one of the rarest of the rare, all the way from Australia, something most of you will have never seen before—outside of children's cartoons, I've been told—an actual Tasmanian devil!"

An animal in a cage was brought in and set on one of the tables. It looked like a ferocious giant rat, with wide open mouth and gleaming teeth.

The presenter was dressed for the Australian outback, in safari clothes and hat. He had a British accent and a cocky manner.

"The Tasmanian devil, ladies and gentlemen, is for those of you who like to live dangerously. This is Rosie. Rosie doesn't like you. Rosie doesn't like anybody. Rosie is a carnivore, and she kills. The Tasmanian devil is endangered because cancer has ravaged the species. Not Rosie, however. Rosie is disease free. Those of you who have brought vets and biologists may take blood samples for testing if you wish. But Rosie is not going to like it, and she's fifteen pounds of fighting fury. She's young, vigorous, healthy, and, frankly, I will be happy not to take her home."

"All right," Fernand said. "Let's start the bidding at ten thousand euros. Do I hear ten thousand?"

A hand went up.

Fernand pointed. "I have ten thousand. Do I hear twenty?"

A hand went up on the other side of the room.

"I have twenty thousand. Do I hear thirty?"

He did. The Tasmanian devil eventually went for seventy-five thousand euros.

Teddy was concerned. If that ugly and insignificant snarling animal went for seventy-five thousand dollars, would a half million be enough for a magnificent black rhino?

He was not to find out. The auction ran long, and the black rhino was held over to the next day. Teddy wondered if that was a ploy to build suspense and drive up the price. There was still time left, but perhaps not enough for a spirited auction.

"So," Fernand said. "I must apologize. I know there are a number of people eager to bid on the black rhino. But it is one auction, I think you will agree with me, that should not be rushed." He smiled. "But there is still time for one special treat. You cannot bid on him. He is not an endangered species, and nothing you would want to hunt. He is, in fact, a hunter's best friend."

There were a few murmurs in the crowd.

"That's right. Allow me to introduce Rocky, short for Rock Star, one of the most talented hunting and herding dogs on the planet. For anyone working with animals, he is invaluable. Ladies and gentlemen, I give you Rocky!"

A handler came out with a dog on a leash. After such a buildup, Rocky was totally unprepossessing. He was a perfectly ordinary large, brown English setter. It was impossible to believe that he was a trained hunting dog. Goofy and lovable was more like it. A family pet. He bounded out with unbridled glee, spun around, and wrenched the leash from the trainer's hand. Delighted to be free, he romped across the room, wagging at the crowd. He reared up on his hind legs, put his paws on Aziz's lap, and tried to lick his face.

It was the first time Teddy had ever seen the little man react. His face showed utter panic, and he dove away from the dog, knocking over the woman from the Chinese contingent as he went.

The trainer was quickly by his side, grabbing the leash, and pulling Rocky away.

Fernand jumped in front of them, putting up his arms and raising his voice. "I'm sorry about that, everyone, but how can you not love that special dog? A brilliant hunting dog, and one of the most lovable animals on the planet. You cannot buy him, but I knew you would admire him."

Aziz did not look like he agreed.

Teddy pressed his cell phone to his ear, faking an urgent phone call. He pushed his way out of the row. Some of the people he climbed over glared at him, but no one was surprised.

The guards let him out while the handler was loading Rocky into a crate.

Teddy went through the lobby and down the hall to the stairway that serviced the underground garage. He knew from Marcel that the majority of the animal transport vehicles were parked on level three. When he emerged onto the floor, he found it packed with trucks and vans, and crates on skids just like the one Rocky had been loaded onto.

Teddy walked out among the cars, took up an inconspicuous position, and waited.

Rocky and his handler were down in five minutes, accompanied by two goons, a pair of steroidal types nearly indistinguishable except for the fact that one had red hair and one had brown. They loaded Rocky's crate into the back of a panel van. The handler got in with him. The goons got in the front seat and started the van.

Teddy smashed the window of an older car that looked like it didn't have an alarm. It didn't. He opened the door, got in, and hot-wired it. He backed up, and pulled out of the space just in time to see the van with Rocky heading up the ramp toward the exit. He pulled out and followed along.

69.

I T FELT RIDICULOUS to tail somebody while wearing a Stetson hat. Teddy took it off and put it on the front seat beside him. He wished he could take off his moustache as well, but removing it with one hand while driving with the other was a recipe for disaster. Teddy scrunched down in the front seat and followed the van.

The van seemed to be headed for Stone Barrington's mews house. Of course, it wasn't. It took a roundabout, made a left turn, and drove away at a ninety-degree angle.

Soon Teddy found himself driving through a residential area in a middle-class neighborhood. After about a mile they came to a modest two-story frame house, with slanting ceilings and dormers. There was no garage. The van pulled into the driveway and parked.

Teddy stopped half a block behind.

The handler got out of the van with the dog on a leash. Rocky bounded happily around the front lawn, marking his territory, and sniffing whatever messages any other dog might have left. It was a small yard; still, the process took forever. Rocky clearly wanted to do a thorough job.

While Rocky was playing, the goons carried the crate in the front door. They came out just as he was finally done. Rocky nearly knocked them down in his eagerness to get inside.

The handler followed the dog into the house. He locked the door behind him, leaving the muscle outside.

The brown-haired goon flopped down in a chair on the porch. The red-haired one set off around the house. Teddy kept him in sight as best he could from the vantage point of half a block away.

On the side of the house was a row of garbage cans and what was obviously a kitchen door. The redhead went up the short steps and tried the knob. It was locked. He continued with his circuit of the house. A few minutes later he emerged from the other side.

Red sat down, and the two goons jabbered away in some language that Teddy was too far away to catch. Red got up, got in the van, and drove off. Brown stayed on the porch.

Teddy started his car and followed the van.

Red drove about ten blocks away to a little bistro. He went in and bought sandwiches and two bottles of beer. He came out, got in the van, and drove back to the house.

Red sat down, and gave a sandwich and a beer to Brown. Brown said something derogatory about the beer, probably that they shouldn't drink on the job. He opened it, however, and used it to wash down his sandwich.

Minutes later, a car drove up and stopped in the driveway.

A little man with a black satchel got out. He had a

stern face and round wire-rimmed glasses. He marched through the front door without so much as a glance at the two bodyguards.

The two men looked at each other, snorted in derision, and went back to their lunch.

While the goons were occupied on the front porch, Teddy crept around the side of the house to the kitchen and eased his way up the creaky steps to the back door.

The kitchen door was flimsy, old, and made of wood. The top half had windowpanes, but a blind had been pulled down in front of them. It was slightly askew, so Teddy could see in the crack.

The dog crate was set up in one corner. Rocky was in the crate.

The little man had set down his black bag and was taking the handler to task. Teddy could hear what he was saying through the cracks in the door.

"So," the little man said. The eyes behind the thick-lensed glasses were cold. "You took him out?"

"I was supposed to let people see him."

"You had him perform?"

"No. Just to look at. I put him right back."

"He didn't jump around? He didn't pull at the leash?"

The little man waved his hand to cut off the reply. "Let's see how much harm you did. Take him out."

The handler snapped the leash on Rocky and opened the crate. Teddy could tell he was trying very hard not to let the dog jump, while not appearing to tug on his collar.

"Put him on the table."

The handler went to pick up the dog.

"Wait."

The little man popped open his bag. He took out a bottle of alcohol and wiped down the tabletop. It was white porcelain, and it gleamed.

The handler lifted Rocky onto the table.

"Turn him over."

That wasn't so easy. Rocky struggled while the handler got him on his side, subdued him in a firm hold, and rolled him onto his back.

"Pull his hairs apart."

The handler spread the long brown hair on Rocky's stomach. "Don't you shave the incision?"

"Not if you don't want it to be discovered. Pull them back."

The handler parted the hairs.

The little man examined the dog's stomach. Underneath the hair, Rocky had a fresh surgical scar running down his belly. The sutures were still in place.

The little man snorted angrily. "He's torn a stitch!"

"Not because I took him out," the handler protested. "The dog is wild."

"Enough! Hold him tight. He's not going to like this."

The little man took a suture kit out of his bag, and leaned over the dog. Rocky howled and squirmed.

"Let him up."

Rocky stood up on the table and shook.

"I'll have to report this," the little man said. He began gathering up his equipment.

Teddy slipped away from the window and stole across the neighbor's lawn to his car. He slid in behind the wheel and settled down to wait.

The little man was out five minutes later. Teddy gave him a head start, and then followed him back to town.

He drove around the outskirts of Paris to a commercial zone where there were more factories than houses. Five miles later, he turned into the parking lot of a strip mall. He drove to the far end of the lot and pulled into a parking spot.

Teddy parked two rows away, got out, and followed him. The little man went into a building marked Kelso Labs.

Teddy would have loved to follow him, but the last thing in the world he wanted was for people to remember some Texan snooping around. Coupled with the fact he was driving a stolen car with a smashed driver's-side window, it was too iffy a prospect.

Teddy drove back to l'Arrington, ditched the car in the garage fairly close to the space he'd stolen it from, and went up to his room. He took out his laptop, and did a search for Kelso Labs.

Kelso Labs was a research facility for 21st Century Pharmaceuticals, a drug company noted for its advances in modern medicine. Nearly sixty percent of their product consisted of innovations in the field of drugs.

Naysayers pointed out that the majority of these "innovations" in pharmacology were merely small variations on existing formulas allowing the same drugs to be rebranded, repackaged, and repriced, with as much as a thousand percent markup. Such complaints seemed to have little effect on the company, whose worth continued to skyrocket.

Twenty-first Century Pharmaceuticals was a wholly owned subsidiary of R & D Enterprises, a multibillion-dollar corporation presided over by René Darjon.

Teddy scrolled back to Kelso Labs and did a search for research scientists. The only ones listed were administrative types and low-level lab assistants.

He tried 21st Century Pharmaceuticals. Minutes later he was staring at a picture of the little man he'd been following.

Dr. Stephan von Heinrich was a third-generation German whose grandfather, Klaus von Heinrich, had come to France at the end of war. Exactly which side he had been on was a little murky. There seemed to have been a decided lack of interest, probably due to the fact he was a physicist rumored to have been working on nuclear fission.

Klaus von Heinrich's son had been a schoolteacher, and barely rated a mention, but his grandson had inherited the family gene.

Dr. Stephan von Heinrich was a renowned research scientist, with degrees in microbiology and virology.

70.

TEDDY HAD PIECES of information now, and he didn't like the way they were adding up. The auction of the endangered animals, disgusting as it was, was irrelevant, an illicit cover for something even deeper. The real auction was all about the dog.

Rocky—clearly no real hunting dog—was being housed with a handler and guarded by two thugs. He'd been operated on by a noted virologist, and a ruthless killer was terrified of him. Despite what the auctioneer had said, he would be sold sometime during the conference.

The Syrians meant to buy him, and it was important enough to them that they had set up a mole in the Paris office to make sure there would be no CIA interference.

The transaction was also important enough that a man such as the Silver Fox was involved.

But was René Darjon involved with the Syrians? Or was he just in it for the money?

Teddy took out a burner phone and called Jacques.

"The Silver Fox."

"What about him?"

"Does he have any political leanings?"

"Such as?"

"Anything that might make him sympathetic to terrorist causes?"

"Are you kidding me?"

"I wish I were. Does he have any connections?"

"Not at all. He's a Frenchman, born and bred. He's only interested in anything that would further him or his industries. Politics doesn't come into it."

"You said funding the conference was out of character for him. Is that just because he's selfish?"

"He's also low on cash."

"Oh?"

"He's had a number of financial reversals in the last few years. His corporation is rumored to be hemorrhaging money. Does that help?"

"I'm afraid it does."

Teddy hung up the phone thinking hard. Kristin had made a play for René Darjon while following Workman's trail, thinking Workman had been investigating the Syrians. But there was no reason for her to believe the Silver Fox was personally involved. He was, but not with the Syrians. He had produced and was selling a deadly virus entirely for personal gain.

René Darjon was the head of a whole separate operation that needed to be shut down.

The situation was even worse than Teddy had feared, and he needed backup. It couldn't be the CIA because Lance still thought there was a mole in the Paris office, and Teddy didn't want to disillusion him before he'd handled this situation. By rights it should be the French police, but Teddy had no in with them, and he had no concrete information to give. Any explanation would be so convoluted he would be dismissed as a kook, treated as a menace, pegged as a suspect, and clapped in jail at the slightest provocation.

Teddy took out a burner phone and called Dino. He reached him at the office of the New York City police commissioner

"Well," Dino said. "Who can this be? It can't be anyone I know because it's from Paris, and everyone I know left Paris."

"How do you know the call's from Paris?"

"I'm the police commissioner. You think I don't screen my calls."

"It's a burner phone."

"It's a burner phone in Paris. I can't trace it to you, but I can pinpoint the city."

"I'll keep that in mind," Teddy said. "You weren't that happy about leaving Paris, were you? That's why you're giving me a hard time."

"I'm giving you a hard time? I wasn't aware of it."

"How would you like to come back?"

"What?"

"It turns out I could use your help."

"You need another apartment rented?"

"There's no real estate involved. This is a job for the police."

"The French police?"

"They're not apt to be receptive. You, on the other hand, have just the right amount of skepticism."

"It's that bad?"

"It's worse."

"Should I get Stone?"

"No. We're doing this under the radar. No Stone. No Mike Freeman. I'd like to keep this as quiet as possible. There's a number of people who shouldn't know."

"Does that include Lance?"

"I have a problem with Lance. Actually, I have several problems with Lance, but one in particular. If he knew what I was up to, he'd probably bring me home."

"You don't have to go."

"Yeah, but I need his backing. And I don't need him making waves. So, are you up for it?"

"Can you tell me what you want me to do?"

"Not over the phone."

"I like it already. Okay. I'll book a flight to Paris and a room at l'Arrington."

"You won't be able to get a room. It's all booked up for the conference."

"The conference?"

"Yeah. The hotel's booked solid all week. I'm not sure even Stone could get in."

"Where are you staying?"

"L'Arrington."

"Of course," Dino said dryly. "You want me in the apartment I rented?"

"Probably not a good idea."

"So where should I go?"

"Why don't you stay at Stone's house? I'm sure he wouldn't mind."

"Can I ask him?"

"Of course you can. Just tell him it's a clandestine op and not to spread it around."

"You're kidding, right?"

"Only half."

71.

TEDDY HAD NO problem buying the black rhino. He easily outbid the Germans, who talked a good game but dropped out after three hundred thousand. Only an Italian nobleman put up much of a fight. Teddy shut him up by jumping the bid up to five hundred thousand. In retrospect, he probably could have gotten it for four, but he figured Lance wouldn't mind.

A winner's boastful bravado was right in Floyd Maitland's wheelhouse. Teddy marched up to the Syrians waving his drink and declared in a loud voice, "So! Did you see who took the black rhino? I have to tell you, it's been one beautiful day. Have a drink on me. That's how it is back home. Losers lick their wounds, and the winners buy drinks. Hey, barkeep! Another round for my buddies."

Fahd grabbed his elbow. "You will keep your voice down," he said tersely. "You will not talk about the panel outside the panel, or I will report you. And there will be consequences."

Teddy waved it away. "Oh, sure, sure. Quiet as a mouse." He draped his arm around Fahd's shoulders as

if they were best friends, and lowered his voice conspira-
torially. "When can we buy the dog?"

"You cannot buy the dog."

"Of course I can. If you have money, you can buy
anything. So when can we bid on him?"

"Did you not hear me? The dog is not for sale."

"I know. The dog is only for special people. People
with money. That would be me. That would be you. You
couldn't outbid me for the rhino. Think you can outbid
me for the dog?"

"You are drunk. You make no sense," Fahd said. He
deliberately turned his back.

Teddy gave up without learning when the dog would
be sold, but Fahd's answers had told him two things: there
was such an auction, and Fahd didn't want him at it.

72.

Dino looked around Teddy's bare, depressing apartment. "I love what you've done with the place."

"Yeah. I keep meaning to decorate, but I've been busy."

"Who are you, now? Fenton Towne? That's the guy I rented the apartment for."

"No, actually I'm Devon Billingham."

"Who's that?"

"The guy with the Paris bank account. He also has a room at the St. Pierre."

"Why can't I stay there?"

"You can get a room there, if you want, but you can't stay in mine. The hotel staff is already wondering why I rented it."

"Why *did* you rent it?"

"To keep my equipment in their safe. There's nowhere here I feel comfortable leaving it."

"I can understand that."

"So who knows you're here?"

"Stone Barrington."

"Anyone else?"

"Just my wife."

"Viv knows you went to Paris?"

"She doesn't know why."

"Well, don't feel so virtuous for not telling her. *You* don't know why."

"She wouldn't tell anyone."

"She works for Mike Freeman."

"Even him." Dino cocked his head. "So, why can't you let Lance in on this?"

"He wouldn't approve of my mode of operation."

"Would I?"

"I doubt it."

"Why not?"

"Probably the body count."

Dino gave him a look.

"Relax. There's no collateral damage here. There's no one who didn't deserve it."

"Why wouldn't Lance be okay with that?"

"It would take too long to explain to his satisfaction. By then the whole thing would have gotten away from me."

"What's this all about?"

Teddy smiled. "Where to begin? Do you know a man named René Darjon?"

"The Silver Fox?"

"Why does everyone know that but me?"

"I'm the commissioner of police in New York City. You work in motion pictures."

"Good point. I've been out of the loop. I liked being out of the loop."

"What about René Darjon?"

"He's one end of the operation."

"How is he involved?"

"He owns the dog."

Dino blinked.

Teddy filled him in on what he knew, and what he thought. It took close to a half hour.

When Teddy was done, Dino took a big breath. "How do you know all this?"

"I don't know all this. A lot of it I just surmise."

"You think René Darjon invented a deadly virus in his research labs? You think he used it to create a biological weapon, and plans to sell it in the midst of an illicit auction hidden in a conservation convention? The prospective buyers include Russia, Syria, China, and Palestine."

"That's the gist."

"You don't think this merits being brought to Lance's attention?"

"He'd never act on an unfounded series of hunches. He'd send out reconnaissance teams and wind up blowing the whole operation. The CIA is fine, in a bull-in-a-China-shop sort of way, but they can't possibly infiltrate this convention without standing out like sore thumbs. I'm already inside. If anyone's got a chance of keeping that virus out of the hands of our enemies, it's me. So I'm not turning the operation over to some well-meaning suit who doesn't know what he's doing."

"What do you need me for?"

"I can't handle both ends of the operation. I have my eye on the buyers. I need you to handle the sellers. Specifically, René Darjon. I need you to nail René Darjon. I want his biological weapons laboratory out of commission."

"You want me to catch the Silver Fox?"

"Of course not. You have no authority. It would have to be the French police."

"You want me to talk to the prefect?"

"I thought you might have lunch."

"I see," Dino said. "You got me here under false pretenses."

"Why do you say that?"

"You don't want me to do something, you want me to be a messenger boy. You have a story you can't tell the police because it would sound like the ravings of a lunatic. So you want *me* to tell the story to the police so *I* sound like a raving lunatic."

"Not at all."

"Why not?"

"Because you're not going to tell them that story."

"What am I going to tell them?"

"I'll think of something."

"You want me to lie to the police?"

"No, I want you to tell them a simplified version of the truth that will make sense and they'll believe. Then you can get them to arrest the Silver Fox."

"They're not going to take kindly to an American policeman showing up and telling them their job."

Teddy smiled. "That depends on how you phrase it."

73.

PARIS PREFECT Clement Moreau smiled at Dino across the table of the elegant five-star café where they were having brunch. "This is purely a social call?"

"Yes and no."

"Tell me about the 'no.'"

"I am here on vacation. My doctor actually advised me to take a break. He said the office of police commissioner is not conducive to my health."

"I get the same thing from my wife. She says the job is taking years off my life."

"Do you agree with her?"

"Absolutely. She's one hundred percent right, which makes her hard to argue with. She is hard enough to argue with when she is one hundred percent wrong."

Dino grinned. "I share your pain."

"You were telling me why you are here."

"I'm here to see you. I was telling you the part of my visit that is not entirely social."

"Always the diplomat."

"So?"

"What is that part?"

The waiter came and set their quiches in front of them.

"I'll have another Parisienne," Dino said.

"Two."

Dino dug in with his fork.

The prefect held up his hand. "Remember the last time you had Quiche Alsacienne?"

The last time Dino took a large bite of the Gruyère and onion quiche he wound up chugging his Parisienne in a vain attempt to cool his scalded throat. Reminded, he carved out a small bite of quiche, and let it sit on the fork to cool.

"So, what can I do for you?" Moreau said.

Dino grimaced. "Like I said, I'm here on vacation. My wife practically forced me to go. She would be very upset if I were to become involved in any police action while I am here."

"I understand."

"A crime is about to be committed. Ordinarily, I would like to work with you to stop it, but I don't want a divorce. I want to go home to my wife and give her a chance to show me how pleased she is with me for keeping out of trouble."

He smiled. "I can see how you would."

"That's why I'm asking you for this favor. I need you to keep my name out of this entirely. As far as the media is concerned, the case was uncovered by you and your department."

"You expect media involvement?"

"I'm afraid it's unavoidable. The arrest is going to make news. You will be pestered for interviews."

"Hmm." The prefect considered the prospect. It did not displease him. "Well, if I must, I must. Why is this such a high-visibility case?"

"Because of the man you will be arresting."

"And who is that?"

"René Darjon."

74.

TEDDY SKIPPED THE wine and cheese tasting. He stopped by the ballroom just long enough to make sure the Syrians were all there, and to lift Fahd's room key. If Fahd had disliked the obnoxious American already, he positively hated the man now after Teddy had pretended to drunkenly stumble into him to pick his pocket. It was risky, but worth it. Teddy could have picked the lock, but he didn't want to spend any more time than he had to getting in dressed as Floyd Maitland.

Teddy took the elevator up to the sixteenth floor, walked down the hall, and swiped the plastic key over the lock. The door clicked open.

He knew at once someone was there. He'd been quiet with the door. With luck, they hadn't heard him. Teddy slipped his gun out of his shoulder holster, and flattened himself against the wall. He peered around the corner.

A woman sat at Fahd's desk. His laptop was open in front of her. As Teddy watched, she opened his e-mails and scrolled through the messages.

Teddy sucked in his breath.

It was Kristin.

He was furious at her. Why should she put her life in danger? Why should she take such a risk? It was not lost on him that it was the very thing he was about to do himself. Even so, didn't she know any better?

Apparently not. The best he could do now was make sure she didn't get killed and keep her from blowing the operation.

Teddy eased himself out of the room, and gently closed the door. So, that confirmed his theory. René Darjon was just the means to an end. Unfortunately, Kristin was determined to spy on the Syrians. And there was nothing Teddy could do about it. Except keep her from getting caught.

Teddy walked back down the hall, and took up a position halfway between the elevators and the room. If Fahd came back, Teddy would have to head him off.

Five minutes later he heard the elevator arrive. He turned and walked toward it. A couple came out of the elevator. It was no one he knew, so he walked on by, and waited at the elevator until they went into their room. Then he went back and took up his position again.

There came the sound of a door opening from the other direction. Teddy turned, and walked back toward Fahd's room.

Kristin came out and headed for the elevator. He passed right by her, but she barely noticed him at all. She clearly had something on her mind.

As soon as she was out of sight, Teddy went back to Fahd's room and unlocked the door.

Fahd's briefcase was open on the table. Teddy searched

it quickly, looking for any reference to the dog. There were none.

Teddy sat down at the computer and looked over the e-mails Kristin had been reading. None were significant. He scrolled through, looking for correspondence about the dog.

He found it in an e-mail sent that very afternoon. He almost missed it because it had no subject line, but he clicked on it and the message opened up.

The message in itself made no sense. It was obviously a continuation of a series of e-mails dealing with the subject. If so, they had been deleted.

The message read in its entirety:

Nine AM. Skin Game.

75.

IT WASN'T MUCH to go on, but Teddy figured there was only one thing it could be. At a quarter to nine the next morning, he put on his cowboy gear and moseyed on down to the panel room.

Two large security guards were stationed at the door. Neither had a clipboard in his hand, like they had for the panels.

Teddy slipped into the men's room down the hall and watched from the vantage point of the door.

At five minutes to nine, the Syrians came down the hall and stopped in front of the panel door. Fahd said something to one of the security guards. He stepped aside and let them in.

The Chinese were next, followed by the Palestinians and the Russians. All were allowed to enter.

When they were all inside, Teddy left the men's room and walked up to the panel door.

The security guard gave no sign of welcome. His face was neutral. "Yes?" he said.

Teddy didn't miss a beat. "Skin game."

The security guard stepped aside and opened the door.

Teddy walked in and surveyed the room.

The Syrians, Russians, Chinese, and Palestinians were seated in the audience. No other groups were represented.

Fahd saw Teddy. His mouth fell open. He sprang to his feet and came over to confront him. "What are you doing here?"

Teddy smiled. "I would imagine the same thing you are."

"You were not invited."

Teddy shrugged. "I got in, didn't I?"

Teddy could practically see Fahd's blood pressure rising as he fought to maintain his composure. "Do not oppose me. You don't care about this. You just want to win."

Teddy grinned his good-ol'-boy grin. "Well, now, everyone likes to win."

"This is not a game," Fahd said. "Do not treat it like a game. If you persist, you will be sorry."

"Is that a threat?" Teddy said good-naturedly. "Hey, calm down there, star buddy. We're all just havin' fun."

Fahd glared at him in helpless frustration, then stomped back to his seat. In contrast, Teddy flopped lazily onto a chair and stretched out comfortably.

Fernand took the lectern. "My friends. You are the chosen few. Up till now, you did not know who the others were. You are here because you got an e-mail. Now you know who else did. Forget that you know. As far as you are concerned, you are the only one here.

"We all know why we are here. It is the reason we came. Once again, I give you Rocky!"

Rocky was wheeled into the room in a crate. The handler opened the crate and let Rocky out. He was careful this time to make sure the dog didn't get away. He led Rocky up and down without incident, and returned him to the crate. The two goons took up positions on either side of it.

"And now, I would like to introduce Dr. Stephan von Heinrich, renowned microbiologist and research scientist, who can explain to you why this dog is so invaluable. Dr. von Heinrich?"

Dr. von Heinrich's hair was slicked back, and his tie looked uncomfortably tight. Teddy got the impression he would be much more at home in a lab coat, bending over his microscope.

"I have engineered a super virus. It is deadly, contagious, and unstoppable."

Dr. von Heinrich pointed to the dog. "The dog is a mule." Heinrich smiled unpleasantly at the poor joke. "Smugglers carry drugs inside them in balloons. Rocky carries the virus in a small vial, sewn into the lining of his stomach in a surgical operation. And it can only be removed by another surgical operation." He shrugged. "Unless the survival of the dog is of no real importance."

Fernand rushed to take the lectern back. Though apparently fine with mass murder, dog killing was not the type of upbeat image he was eager to promote.

"I think Dr. von Heinrich has established the value of the dog. In a moment I will open the bidding. Before I do, I have one more point to make.

"You all know this from the invitation, but I will

repeat it one more time, just so there can be no confusion. If you win the bid, you will not take possession of the dog. The dog will remain with us under our strict security measures until the conference is over. At which time, the dog will be delivered to you at the airport and loaded into your private plane. That is why anyone bidding on the dog was required to have a private plane. The dog must be flown out of the country. Intact. Under no condition may the vial be removed from the dog within the borders of France. Is that clear?

"To anyone for whom that is not clear, or who does not wish to abide by those rules, please refrain from bidding."

Fernand clapped his hands together. "So, let us begin! We will open the bidding at one million euros."

Teddy's mouth fell open. Of course, that was in keeping with Floyd Maitland's image. He threw in a "Hey ya!" as a sound effect.

Everyone glared at him. After all, he was a bugaboo, the insane bidder they had to beat.

Fahd took advantage of the distraction to seize the first bid. "One million."

"I have one million over here."

"Two million." From the Russians.

"Three."

"Four."

The Palestinians and the Chinese chimed in in rapid succession.

"I have four million, do I hear—"

"Ten," said Fahd.

"Twenty." From the Russians.

"Fifty." From the Chinese.

There was a brief respite while people retrenched.

"I have fifty million. Do I hear—"

"Seventy-five." From Fahd.

"Eighty." From the Russians.

Teddy smiled. It was a show of weakness, a raise of only five million. The Russians weren't going to last.

The Chinese bumped it up to a hundred million, and they were off to the races.

When the smoke finally cleared, the dog went for 275 million dollars. Teddy had a feeling it would have gone for more, but everyone was just waiting for him to jump in with a bid. And while they were waiting, the bidding was closed.

The Syrians won the dog.

Teddy was not at all surprised.

76.

LANCE WAS NOT pleased to see Millie, even if this time she came to him. He walked up to her on the lawn and said sardonically, "So, are we talking seven figures?"

"He doesn't want any money."

"Really? I wouldn't have thought you could surprise me anymore, but you just did. What does he want?"

"A dog."

Lance gave her the most marvelous deadpan. "What?"

"He needs you to find a dog and a handler and get them on a plane to Paris at once. Mike Freeman will supply the aircraft. You just have to get the dog."

"He really needs a dog?"

"Yes."

"Why can't he get his own dog?"

"It has to look like this."

Millie held up her cell phone so Lance could see the attached photo Teddy had texted her.

"First he wants a rhino, now he wants a dog?"

"That's it in a nutshell."

"And what is the dog for?"

"He hasn't told me."

"I assume it's to catch the mole. He does realize *mole* is a figure of speech."

Millie smiled.

Lance eyes narrowed. "He said I'd say that?"

"You two seem to be in mind-meld. Put your best men on it. This is a high-priority, need-to-know, eyes-only op. Under no circumstances does it leak to anyone at the French embassy."

"He hasn't found the mole."

Millie smiled.

Lance looked pained. "He knew I'd say that, too?"

"He told me to say: 'Did you think it was going to be easy?'"

77.

Dino drove up to the St. Pierre in an SUV. Teddy opened the door and hopped in.

"So," Dino said. "You promised I wouldn't be renting apartments, so you got me renting cars."

"It's a clandestine op," Teddy said. "You gonna gripe about bringing equipment?"

"What are *you* bringing?"

"What do you mean?"

"You had me pick you up at the St. Pierre dressed as Devon Billingham. I assume you went to the hotel safe."

"Exactly. You got your equipment, I got mine."

"What's your equipment?"

"That's on a need-to-know basis."

"Are you trying to be irritating?"

"It's nice to tweak a police commissioner."

"I can imagine it would be."

"Any problem with the paperwork?"

"Not at all. The prefect is happy to have me work behind the scenes, as long as I don't take any of the credit. I have his authorization to bring a dog into the country without any of the usual bullshit."

"What did you tell him it is?"

"A drug-sniffing dog."

"Good cover."

They got to the airport about a half hour before the Strategic Services jet touched down.

Teddy recognized the first man off the plane as one of Mike Freeman's agents, but the agent didn't recognize him.

He recognized Dino, though. He grinned. "You're Dino Bacchetti."

"No, I'm not," Dino said. "And don't make me get Mike Freeman to remind you."

The agent gulped. "My mistake, sir. Do you have authorization to receive the package?"

"Good man," Dino said. He handed him the papers.

The agent scanned the papers and handed them back. He called to the plane, "Send him down."

A man came down the steps with a dog on a leash. The dog couldn't wait to get off the plane, and was practically pulling the handler over. The dog hit the runway, sniffing in all directions, and hurried to pee on the luggage cart.

Once the dog had calmed down, Teddy performed the introductions. The handler was Gary. The dog was Barkley. Teddy introduced himself as Devon and Dino as Jake. He figured Dino would like that.

Mike Freeman's men unloaded a dog crate from the plane and set it up in the back of the SUV. Barkley was used to the crate, and jumped right in. The men loaded the handler's suitcase and a bag of dog food in next to the crate. The handler got in the car, and they took off.

Dino drove back and pulled up in front of Teddy's apartment.

"Okay," Teddy said, "let's get you situated."

Teddy and the handler got out. Teddy popped the back of the SUV and took out the suitcase and dog food.

"What about Barkley?" the handler said.

"We have to check him out. He'll be up in a little while."

"I should stay with him."

Teddy cocked his head. "Did they give you specific instructions to do everything I told you?"

"Yes."

"You stay here."

Teddy took the handler upstairs and set him up in the apartment.

"Hey, there's no TV," the handler said.

"Did they tell you to bring a book?"

"Yes."

"Read it."

Teddy went down and hopped in the car with Dino.

"Was he giving you trouble?" Dino asked.

"He didn't want to leave his dog."

"Can you blame him?"

From the back of the car, Barkley, who realized he wasn't being let out, whimpered plaintively.

"I know how you feel," Dino said, as they drove off.

78.

IT WAS NEARLY midnight when they arrived at the house. Dino parked around the corner and killed the lights and motor.

Teddy and Dino approached the house from a neighbor's property that was blocked off by a hedgerow. Over it they could see the top half of the front door. One of the goons was sitting on the porch.

"Okay," Teddy said. "Wait here."

"'Wait here'?" Dino said. "Really?"

"It's not enough to aid and abet, you want to kill the guard yourself?"

"You're going to kill him?"

"I hope not. It wouldn't serve my purpose." Teddy reached in his gear bag and took out a tube, slightly larger than a soda straw.

"What's that?" Dino said.

"It's a blowpipe. Designed it myself. Accurate up to twenty-five feet. I need to knock out the guards without them knowing I was here." Teddy snapped open a little case and took out two darts. He took out a third. "Margin of error," he told Dino.

Teddy snuck up on the house, keeping to the shadows, his footfalls nearly silent on the grass. The guard on the front porch was Red. He wasn't sleeping, but he might as well have been.

Teddy crept around to the side of the house. Brown was stationed at the kitchen door. He wasn't paying attention, either, and posed an easier target. Teddy crept up on him, raised the blowpipe, and fired. The dart hit the goon in the side of the neck. He reacted as if he'd been bitten by a mosquito, and slapped at it. He missed. His head lolled to the side, and he was out.

Teddy retrieved the dart and peered around the corner of the house at the goon on the front porch. He hadn't moved, but he was thinking deep thoughts, probably about women or gambling.

Red was right on the edge of the blowpipe's range. Teddy figured he could make it, but preferred to get closer.

A twig snapped underfoot.

The goon raised his head and looked around.

The dart hit him in the cheek. Not where Teddy was aiming, but the guy had moved.

The mission was blown if the guy saw him. The mission was blown if he even noticed the dart.

He didn't. He started to get up and sank back down, slid sideways, and pitched off the chair with a crash.

Teddy rushed to the porch, grabbed him by his shoulders, and heaved him back up into the chair—it had to look like he'd fallen asleep, not as if he'd been drugged. Teddy's bad leg hurt, but he barely noticed. He propped up the goon, and faded back into the shadows, waiting to see if a light went on in the house.

None did. Teddy gave it a couple of minutes, and went back up on the porch.

The front door was locked. It took Teddy twenty seconds to pick it. Was he rusty, out of shape, or just old? Whatever the case, a refresher course in lock picking was in his future.

The door creaked as he slipped inside and pulled it closed behind him. He couldn't see a thing. He had a penlight, but hated to use it. He stood for a minute and let his eyes adjust to the dark. Shapes began to take form. To some extent he was extrapolating from where he stood in the doorway. There was a room directly in front of him and doors off in either direction. He also had a clue from the guards. He knew approximately where the kitchen was.

Teddy aimed the penlight at the floor in front of him, cupping his hand to narrow the beam. He made his way through the door to the right and down the hallway to the kitchen.

He was greeted by the sound of a dog stirring in his crate. He prayed it wouldn't bark. Rocky didn't. Rocky was no watchdog. Wagging and greeting was more in his line.

Teddy reached the kitchen door and peered in. Rocky was in a crate in the corner. Teddy tiptoed to the crate, treats in hand. Rocky slurped them gratefully through the bars.

Teddy didn't see a leash anywhere, but he'd brought

one of his own. He slipped it on Rocky's collar through the bars of the crate. Having seen Rocky in action, Teddy wasn't sure he could get a leash on him if he let him out first.

Teddy took a breath, and opened the crate. Rocky came out in a whoosh. Teddy held him fast and fed him treats from his pocket. It took Rocky a minute to realize he was doing just fine for himself standing still. Of course, it wouldn't take him long to remember he had to pee.

Teddy worked his way across the kitchen and out the door, leash and penlight in one hand, treats in the other. He reached the front door, eased it open, and followed the dog out. He closed the door, but left it ajar.

Rocky made a break for the lawn, pulling Teddy off the porch. He followed the dog to the side of the lawn, where Rocky peed on a bush.

Dino loomed up out of the dark. "Need a hand?" he whispered.

"Give me the spare collar."

Dino held Rocky while Teddy snapped the new collar they'd brought around his neck, clipped the leash to it, then unsnapped Rocky's original collar.

"Okay," Teddy said. "You guys are set, I'll meet you back at the car."

Dino took the leash and led Rocky off, or rather Rocky led him.

Teddy hurried back around the corner to the SUV, where Barkley was sitting alertly in his crate. Teddy opened the crate door and slipped Rocky's collar around his neck. Barkley jumped out, sniffing the air. Clearly he smelled another dog, but Dino had led Rocky far enough away that it wasn't a problem. Teddy was able to distract Barkley with treats, and led him to the front door.

Teddy eased the door open, snapped on the penlight beam, and made his way to the kitchen. Barkley was happy to go. He seemed more manageable than Rocky. Teddy wondered if the handler would notice.

The crate door was open. Barkley walked right in. Teddy unsnapped the leash, tossed Barkley a few treats to keep him happy, and turned to go.

A light came on in the house.

Teddy could hear the sound of footsteps coming down the stairs from the second floor.

The stairs were between the kitchen and the foyer, so Teddy couldn't get out. There was the kitchen door, but the goon's chair was blocking it.

There was a pantry off the kitchen. Not a full pantry, just an alcove with shelves and no door. Teddy slipped in, and tried to flatten himself against the side wall.

The kitchen light snapped on.

Barkley sprang up, wagging his tail.

The handler stood in the doorway. "I'm not taking you out again. I just took you out. You need to settle down. I'll give you a treat, and you lie down. That's the deal. Take it or leave it."

The handler took a treat from a paper bag on the table, walked over, and held it out for the dog. Barkley slurped it gratefully, wagged his tail, sat, and waited for another.

Teddy held his breath. If sitting for a treat wasn't one of Rocky's behaviors, the handler would notice. And Teddy's right shoulder was visible in the pantry alcove, if the handler glanced in that direction.

The handler looked the crate up and down as if something seemed to be different. He must have decided there wasn't. He frowned, shrugged, turned to go.

The dog barked.

The handler turned back and put up his hand, palm out. "Rocky. Stay."

It was a universal dog command. Barkley knew it, too. He stopped complaining and accepted the fact that he was being left. The handler gave him one last look and switched off the light.

Teddy breathed again. He stuck his head out from the pantry alcove and listened to the handler's footsteps heading down the hall. The stairs creaked as he plodded up them.

The upstairs light went out. Teddy gave it another minute. The handler was probably still awake, but Teddy had to get moving. At least this time he wasn't taking a dog. He switched on the penlight to make sure he wouldn't knock anything over, and made his way to the front door. He eased it open, slipped out, and shut it gently behind him.

The goon was still sitting on his chair, looking to all intents and purposes like a guard who'd fallen asleep at his post. Teddy hurried across the lawn to the car.

Dino started the engine and pulled out. "I saw lights go on in the house. Did you wake the handler?"

"Barkley woke the handler. He wasn't keen on being left alone."

"Is he going to give the game away?"

"I didn't have time to teach him his lines."

Dino drove back to the apartment. Teddy went in and got the dog handler.

"Be careful taking him out of the crate," Teddy warned. "He's a little hyped up from the tests."

As if to demonstrate, Rocky took a flying leap out of the back of the SUV and tried to hurtle down the street.

"What did you *do* to him?" the handler said, bracing his feet and restraining the dog.

"Don't worry, the drugs will wear off."

"'Drugs'?"

"I'm kidding. He's just glad to see you."

The handler got control of Rocky. He took him for a short walk, brought him back, and went inside, all without noticing he was walking another dog entirely.

Teddy and Dino set up the crate and took off before the handler could ask any more questions.

Teddy smiled at Dino. "Okay, we saved the world from extinction. Let's get the guys who were trying to do it."

79.

TEDDY CALLED MIKE Freeman at his office in New York. "You know who this is?"

"I understand my men didn't. You're very good at what you do."

"Sometimes it's a curse. I need them to do something for me, and they'll have to hear it from you."

"Name it."

"There are some Syrians in Paris for a rare animal convention. Their leader is a strongman named Fahd Kassin. They've got a private plane out at the airport. I need your boys to locate it."

"Without anyone knowing they're looking?"

"That would defeat the whole purpose."

"I figured it would."

"Will that be a problem?"

"Hell, no. It will give them something to do. Anything else I can do for you?"

"When they find out, it would be nice if they told me. I'd hate to have to call you to get the information."

"No problem. Just tell them *Ice Nine Brushfire*."

"That's the password?"

"It will be."

"How will I know when they have it?"

"Give them a couple of hours. If they haven't found it by then, it isn't there."

80.

TEDDY, DRESSED AS an aviation mechanic, walked down the runway in front of the hangars. Mike Freeman's agents had done a good job. The plane was there, housed in hangar forty-seven, and the pilot in charge of the plane liked to pass the time playing pinochle with the pilots in the hangar next door.

Teddy was pleased to see the game was in full swing. He walked by hangar forty-seven, turned, and walked around toward the back. He would have liked a window, but you can't always get what you want. The walls were solid, with only a small ventilation duct near the roof. The hangar doors were the only way in and out.

It was a coin flip. No one was watching. Did he creep quietly around the corner of the building and slip in the front door, or did he walk by bold as brass and amble in as if he had every right to do so?

The latter seemed the better approach. If seen, he could pretend he'd accidentally entered the wrong hangar. That wouldn't work if he was seen sneaking in.

Teddy walked in purposefully as if he worked there. No one challenged him. They were all playing cards.

The Syrians' plane would have been dwarfed next to the Strategic Services jet. It looked like a twelve seater at best, with none of the amenities. Teddy smiled. He could imagine Fahd being pissed off that he hadn't been given better.

The ladder was in place, and the door was open. Teddy waited to see if there was anyone inside. When he was reasonably certain there wasn't, he climbed the steps and went on board.

Teddy's estimate had been accurate. It appeared there had been six rows of seats, though now there were only five, two to a row, one on each side of the aisle. Teddy crept down the aisle. Sure enough, there on the floor were the holes where the back row had been unbolted and lifted out, probably to make room for a dog crate. Apparently the Syrians had counted on winning the bid.

Teddy heard brisk footsteps as a man came into the hangar, and he ducked down in the plane. He scooted next to a window and peered out quickly.

It was the Syrian pilot, and Teddy was trapped. There was no way he could get out, and no reasonable explanation for why he was there.

He glanced around. There was an access panel in the back of the plane. Teddy made for it, and wrenched it open to find a luggage compartment. He crawled in and pulled the door shut behind him just as the pilot came up the steps to the plane.

Teddy could hear the steps of the pilot coming down the aisle, and realized with dismay that he'd left the hatch ajar. If the pilot noticed, he'd close it. But he'd probably look in first. Would it be dark enough that the man wouldn't see him? Yet another in an endless stream of potential disasters. Teddy scrunched back in the darkness and bumped into the hull.

He saw a crack of light. There was another hatch door. The cargo hold could be accessed from inside or out. He searched for a handle and found one, probably installed to ensure against anyone getting locked inside.

Teddy pushed the hatch open. It was on the opposite side of the passenger door. He squirmed through and dropped to the concrete hangar floor.

The pilot had not investigated the luggage hold. He was just going down the steps. Teddy crouched behind an oil drum until the pilot left the hangar again. He gave it two more minutes, and snuck out.

Teddy sighed and shook his head.

This was not going to be easy.

81.

T EDDY CHECKED HIS messages in the lobby of the St. Pierre. There was an encrypted e-mail from Millie.

Teddy decoded it. It read: Lance wants to know when he can get the dog back. It belongs to a friend of his.

Teddy sent her a message: Prepare the friend for bad news.

Millie e-mailed back: What happened to the dog?

Teddy sent: Nothing yet.

Teddy logged off the computer, cursed Lance, and went to the front desk. "I'm Devon Billingham. I'd like to get my trunk out of the hotel safe."

Teddy had the trunk brought up to his room. After the bellboy had left, he opened it up, took out his equipment bag, and set it on the bed.

He sorted through and selected a few items that he stowed in his jacket pocket. He repacked the trunk, returned it to the desk manager to store in the hotel safe, and strolled back out again.

82.

D INO RETURNED FROM his meeting with the prefect.

"Is everything all set?" Teddy asked.

"Almost."

"What's wrong?"

"He's good on everything except letting the Syrians get away. He wants to arrest them, too."

"I had a feeling he might."

"He'd like to catch them with the dog. That will complete all the links in the chain."

"It would if I hadn't switched dogs. Catching them with Barkley isn't going to be good for anyone. Except Lance. His buddy wants the dog back."

"Are you kidding me?"

"If only." Teddy sighed. "I take it this is a deal breaker?"

"There's no deal to break," Dino said. "The Paris police have all the information. He's going to move on it."

"Okay. Time for a little razzle-dazzle."

"What?"

"A little hocus-pocus. A little bait and switch. A little skin game."

"What do you have in mind?"

"Look. Two out of three's not bad, right?"

"It depends what you're talking about."

"I'm talking about your friend, the prefect of police."

"I thought you were. I'm not going to like this, am I?"

"You're going to love it, and so will he. After all, you're doing him a favor. If he winds up nailing a mad scientist and the Silver Fox, he's not going to feel that bad about the dog. He'll be too busy taking bows to give it any thought."

Dino groaned. "What do I have to do?"

"You have to pull a scam on the prefect."

"I don't think I can do that."

"Sure you can. You just need to keep him from showing up at the airport."

"How?"

"Here's the story. You got a tip from your source that the Syrians are picking up the dog at the handler's house the morning after the conference. If he wants to take out both ends of the operation he should arrest them there. He'll get the Syrians, the dog, and the handler who was housing him.

"At the same time, he hits the scientist's lab and René Darjon's office. He has to do it all at once, so no one is tipped off.

"The beauty of that is he'll want to be personally involved in the arrest of René Darjon. Which means he won't be one of the cops busting an empty house."

"As if that makes it all better," Dino said dryly. "If he doesn't get the dog, there's no connection between René

Darjon and the Syrians—and René Darjon walks. And the scientist walks. And the Syrians get away. Everyone gets away except me. I'll probably get the guillotine."

"I think they stopped using that."

"I'm not eager to find out." Dino spread his arms. "I'm right, aren't I? Without the dog, the prefect's got nothing on René Darjon?"

"That's probably true," Teddy admitted.

"So?"

"So let's get something."

83.

IT TOOK TEDDY forty-five minutes to break into Kelso Labs. The majority of that time was spent disabling the security system. The main system wasn't hard, but they had more backup systems than Fort Knox. Once the last alarm was silenced and the last camera was turned off, it was a simple matter of picking a lock.

Teddy entered through a maintenance door and followed the back hallway to the main corridor. Dr. Stephan von Heinrich's lab was the third door on the left. Just in case there was any doubt, the good doctor had slapped his name on it. He also had locked it more securely than the other labs on the wing.

Teddy made short work of the lock, slipped in, and closed the door. From what he could see in the dim light, Dr. Heinrich had all the latest technological improvements, from electron microscopes to centrifuges, to a device that looked like a CT scanner.

Teddy shone his flashlight beam around. In addition to shelves of tubes and beakers, crates and cages lined the walls. There were no animals in them, but water bowls indicated there had been.

Teddy bypassed all the equipment. He sat at the doctor's desk and switched on his computer. He opened the network folders and scanned the files. None seemed relevant. A global file search for the name *Rocky* came up empty.

Teddy got up from the desk and searched for hard copies. A file cabinet looked like it hadn't been used in years. He checked it anyway. It hadn't. None of the papers in it were current.

Teddy struck pay dirt in the coat closet. He pushed the lab coats aside and discovered a safe.

The safe was a formidable-looking affair, but still no match for Teddy's skill. A few minutes of work and he had the door open.

In the safe were several file folders. Most were of no interest to him, but one was labeled VIRUS X.

Teddy flipped it open. Virus X was a new strain of virus X759C4743P, discovered in the lab by Dr. von Heinrich himself. While the virus was not touted as a biological weapon, its attributes were listed. It was a highly contagious and fatal airborne pathogen.

A subfolder dealt with the surgical procedure on the dog, the insertion of the vial into his stomach, and the sutures anchoring it in place. The removal of the vial was described in detail, with emphasis on maintaining its integrity to ensure against the slightest leak.

Teddy went through the files from top to bottom. Nothing in them implicated René Darjon.

Teddy took the files over to the desk. He skimmed through them again, looking for an appropriate page. He selected one, and fed it into the doctor's scanner. He converted it to a Word document he could edit. After the phrase, "conducted by Dr. Stephan von Heinrich," he added, "under the authorization of René Darjon." He printed it out and compared it to the original. It was perfect.

Teddy stuck the original page in his pocket, replaced it with the altered page, and copied the whole document. He put the original back in the file folder labeled VIRUS X, returned it to the safe, and locked it. He put the full-document photocopy in a blank file folder and took that file with him.

84.

R& D Enterprises was much easier to break into than Kelso Labs. The only trick was timing the rounds of the night watchman to be able to get in and out without being seen. The lock on the front door was a joke, the alarms were turned off because of the watchman, and the security-camera controls were conveniently located behind the reception desk.

René Darjon's offices took up the whole ninth floor. His reception area could have serviced the entire company. It boasted three couches and two large chairs. They weren't the least bit worn. Teddy doubted if they were used much. Reception struck him as the first line of defense. Only the elite few were allowed into the office of his personal secretary.

René Darjon's office was what one would expect of a CEO, from the wooden bar to the flat-screen TV. The desk was a massive oak affair, at once classic and modern. The walls were wood-paneled. The chairs in front of the desk were leather. The lone framed picture behind the desk featured René Darjon receiving an award from the prime minister.

The desk had few drawers, two on the left and one on the right. They held nothing of interest, with the exception of an address book. None of the addresses were of business associates. His secretary doubtless kept track of those. Most of the names seemed to be of young women.

Unfortunately, the desk was not the type of place where René Darjon would have kept anything important. Nor was there any such place in the bar. It would appear that all important papers were kept in the outer office, which was arguably not in his possession, or even under his direct supervision.

Teddy looked at the picture on the wall. An accolade from the prime minister was certainly an honor, but the Silver Fox had undoubtedly received more than his fair share. What was so special about this one?

Teddy had long since learned to follow his hunches. He lifted the painting off the wall, revealing a safe. It was not nearly as good a safe as the one in Dr. von Heinrich's lab, but a safe nonetheless. Teddy had it open in seconds.

It was full of money. Bundles and bundles of hundred-euro notes. There must have been close to a half million euros, just mad money to René Darjon.

Teddy took some of it. Not that he needed the money, he just had to make room in the safe.

Teddy wrote *Virus X* on the file folder in Magic Marker, locked it in the safe, and got out.

85.

TEDDY HADN'T SEEN Kristin in a few days. He was concerned. There were only a few things that could mean: none of them good.

Her cover may have been blown, and she had come to harm. Teddy knew from experience these guys played rough.

Or she could be lying low, waiting to strike at the end of the conference. That could only lead to disaster. Whatever she was plotting was sure to throw a monkey wrench into his plans.

Teddy never once considered the possibility that she might have simply given up. It just wasn't in her nature.

Teddy called Jacques. He caught him at his computer.

"What do you need?"

"Anything going on?"

"It's pretty quiet."

"Anybody at the office show an interest in the conference?"

"None. It's a nonevent. It might as well not be happening."

"Is Kristin around?"

"Norton sent her to London with the ambassador's wife."

"Really?"

"She wasn't happy about it. She tried to foist it off on Valerie but Norton wouldn't let her. He put his foot down. It's no secret he's been getting fed up with her lately. Feels she's grown lax about following orders and has a tendency to do whatever she wants."

"He's not wrong about that. When does she get back?"

"Not until tomorrow. Which takes her out of the picture as far as you are concerned. The conference will be over."

"Right."

"Is that why she was so upset? She was planning to hook up with you?"

"Why do you say that?"

"Well, you two seemed close. And you asked about her."

"I was asking in terms of the conference."

"Of course," Jacques said. "You forget, I'm French."

"Never," Teddy said.

Teddy hung up the phone feeling better. Kristin was out of the way for the rest of the conference. He could imagine the scene in Norton's office. Having managed to establish an off-the-books relationship with René Darjon, Kristin could not have been easy to dissuade.

Teddy couldn't recall ever feeling so nervous about an operation. But that was only natural. He couldn't recall an operation where there had ever been so much at stake.

86.

TEDDY DRESSED UP for the farewell cocktail party in Floyd Maitland's finest cowboy regalia, much like Maitland's standard daily outfit but festooned with bright hand-stitched embroidery. His dinner jacket and blue jeans went together surprisingly well when complemented by his Stetson hat and snakeskin cowboy boots. The only thing missing was his gun belt and Colt revolver. He had no wish to make a scene, merely to come across as a familiar and genial presence.

The grand ballroom was decked out for the party with streamers hanging from the ceiling and animal posters adorning the walls. As in the opening party there were cash bars for liquor and free bars for soft drinks, and a buffet table in the center for finger foods. The fare was better than at the opening party, with such items as shrimp and sliders.

The participants were better dressed, too. While the opening was billed as a "ceremony," this was billed as a "cocktail party," and the guests wore attire fit for the occasion.

Teddy pushed his way through the crowd, hoping to *accidently* bump into the Syrians. He hoped to learn when their plane was leaving. Flush with victory, they might be less guarded.

Teddy saw the Germans, sitting at a table off to the side. They were getting drunk, and it was going to be a morose drunk. After failing to purchase the rhino, they had more or less lost interest in the proceedings. Teddy couldn't recall them bidding on anything else.

The Palestinians didn't look happy, either. Of course, they had lost one of their number, but he was doubtless expendable. They had lost out on the dog, as had the Russians and Chinese. Only the Syrians would be pleased.

Teddy spotted them on the far side of the room. They had also dressed for the party. For Fahd it was a dinner jacket. For the scientists it was ill-fitting suits. The fire-plug hitman wore a suit off the rack, most likely from the plus-size children's department.

Teddy maneuvered close enough to have seen them casually, without actually looking for them. His face lit up in a smile, and he waved and said, "Howdy." He walked over, leaned in, and said in a low voice, "Don't worry, I'm not going to talk loud, but I just have to say it: Congratulations! This has been the best convention ever, hasn't it? Worked out great for both of us."

"Yes," Fahd said, and turned away to cut off the conversation.

Teddy plowed right through the signal. "So when are you taking off? I got a three o'clock flight, but you got your own plane, you can leave anytime you want. When do you leave for the airport?"

Fahd made no attempt to answer, and actually took a step away.

Teddy tried a few more ploys, but it was no use. Now that the convention was done, Fahd saw no reason to even be civil to the obnoxious Texan.

Teddy gave up. There was no help for it, he was just going to have to break into Fahd's room again and search for a note or an e-mail regarding flight time.

Teddy went over to the bar and ordered a drink. Ever careful, he didn't want the Syrians to see him leaving right after his chat with Fahd. An alert spy might notice the correlation, and realize the Texan had come to the party just to talk to them. It was the type of thing Teddy would notice, and anything Teddy could do, he had to assume could be done. The fireplug assassin didn't look very swift, but it was impossible to tell what he thought. It would not hurt to appear social.

Teddy got himself a bourbon on the rocks and headed happily to the snack table, favoring the company with a liberal sprinkling of *comin'-throughs* and *pardon-me-ma'ams*. He reached the finger foods, snagged a pig in a blanket, dipped it in mustard, and popped it in his mouth. "Don't tell me *that's* French," Teddy said, helping himself to another one.

Teddy spotted one of the Syrian scientists at the bar refilling his drink. It was Dr. Chaim, the zoologist, the more compliant of the two.

Teddy set his full drink on the tray of a passing busboy, strode up to the bar, and ordered another bourbon on the rocks. He turned and pretended to see the zoologist for the first time.

"Hey, there, buddy," he said heartily, slapping the zoologist on the shoulder. "Show's over. We all go home tomorrow. What time are you taking off? My plane leaves at three, but you guys got your own plane, don't you?"

Dr. Chaim was in the middle of paying for his drink, but it was not in him to be rude. "Dr. Badim and I are on a commercial flight. It doesn't leave until five."

"Oh, that's a shame. Your buddies will be home by then. Aren't they leaving in the morning?"

"Yes, they leave at eleven."

"Well, you have a safe trip, buddy." Teddy saluted him with his drink, and headed back toward the snack table. Not that he wanted another pig in a blanket, but from there he could see what Fahd was doing.

Teddy was in luck. Fahd's back was turned, and he wasn't paying attention to him at all. Teddy began working his way toward the door.

Kristin came in. She was not dressed for the party, she wore conservative, comfortable clothes, suitable for travel. She had clearly just come from the airport, probably had checked her bags with the concierge. As Teddy watched, she wove her way through the crowd.

Teddy frowned. Was René Darjon here? He hadn't seen him, and the Silver Fox was hardly inconspicuous.

Teddy followed Kristin, keeping parallel to her as she crossed the floor. She was heading toward Fahd, which didn't compute, until she veered off and began weaving a path behind him out of his line of sight.

Had she flown back from London for a new mission involving Fahd?

As she went by, Teddy saw her slip something into the side pocket of Fahd's jacket.

Kristin vanished in the crowd before she could be spotted, let alone identified. Fahd turned to see who had bumped him, but she was gone. He put his hand in his pocket, and came out with a folded piece of paper. He unfolded it, read it to himself. He frowned and took a glance around him. Then he tore it in half, tossed it into a garbage bin, and walked away.

Teddy pushed his way out of the grand ballroom. He reached the lobby in time to see Kristin pull a carry-on bag out the front door. He would have liked to follow her, but he needed to know what the message said.

By the time he returned to the ballroom, the Syrians had made their way across the room. Teddy quickly downed the rest of his bourbon and placed the disposable cup into the garbage can.

Nobody noticed the two tiny slips of paper discreetly tucked in his hand.

TEDDY WALKED TOWARD the men's room, tipping his hat to fellow conference-goers along the way, went in, and closed himself in a stall.

He straightened the crumpled pieces of paper and fit them together.

It was a note:

It's a go. Leave as scheduled.

87.

TEDDY WENT UP to his room and took off his Stetson hat, his cowboy boots, and the rest of his Floyd Maitland outfit. He got out his makeup kit, went in the bathroom, and changed his appearance to that of Agent Felix Dressler. He put on a suit and tie, and his shoulder holster. He slipped his CIA credentials into his pocket, not that he expected to need them, just out of habit.

He went out front and hailed a cab. He got out two blocks from Kristin's apartment building and walked the rest of the way. He breezed through the lobby door as another tenant was leaving, and went upstairs.

Teddy took care not to make a sound picking the lock on the apartment door. He eased it open.

Kirstin stood there holding a gun. Her mouth fell open. "I thought you left."

"I came back."

"What are you doing here?"

"It would appear I'm about to be shot."

Kristin looked at the gun in her hand. "Oh." She lowered it. "Why are you here? I'm pleased to see you, of course, but it's so late. I just got back from London. I was babysitting an ambassador's wife."

"That doesn't sound like you."

"I tried to get out of it. Norton was being a prick."

"I can imagine."

"I'm beat. Could we do this tomorrow?"

"I'm afraid not."

Teddy walked her into the living room, and sat with her on the couch. He gently took the gun from her hand, and laid it on the coffee table.

"What's so urgent?" Kristin said.

Teddy smiled wistfully. "Oh, I think you know."

"Believe me, I haven't got a clue."

"Oh, I think you do. You're very smart. You played me, and not many people can play me."

"I don't know what you're talking about."

"Don't embarrass yourself. You're the mole. You knew I was in Paris to find you. That's why you made a play for me, to learn my game. The first night, you went through my pockets while I was asleep. You found the keys to the train station lockers. You snuck out, searched the lockers, found the passports, and figured out what I was up to.

"You said Workman wasn't interested in you, but any-body could see that wasn't true. You used him, ended your relationship, but kept him dancing on a string. You made a play for him to gather intel, pumped him for in-formation, found out he'd searched one of the lockers. Got him to tell you the name on the passport. Then you got word to the Syrians to start an Internet search for that name, so I'd think Workman was the mole."

"Workman was the mole? He's been missing for days. Is that why?"

"It's no use, Kristin." Teddy took his gun out of his shoulder holster and held it in his lap. "If it's any consolation, you're very good at what you do."

"Not good enough, apparently."

"No one ever is. There's always someone better." Teddy smiled sadly and shook his head. "Why, Kristin, why?"

"You know why."

"I assure you I don't. You were trained by the CIA. How could you betray them?"

"The CIA wanted me to be an errand girl. I wanted to be a spy."

"Oh, come on."

"I met a man in Berlin, on one of my babysitting missions. He was the real deal. He was everything I wanted to be."

"He was on the other side."

"What are sides? It's all a game. Just different uniforms."

"It's not a game, Kristin. These are bad men. You know what they are buying? A deadly virus."

"Why is that so bad? We have warheads. We're not going to use them, but having them makes us strong."

"That's how you justify it?" Teddy shook his head. "James Bond is fiction, Kristin. There's no such thing. But you were very good."

She smiled a sad smile. "I liked you."

"I liked you, too," Teddy said.

Kristin lunged for the gun on the coffee table.

It broke his heart. She must have known it was hopeless. But she couldn't let herself get arrested. It wasn't in her nature. She was a storybook heroine, a romantic to the last. The type of agent who would have swallowed a poison pill, if she'd had one.

She grabbed the gun and aimed.

He pulled the trigger.

88.

TEDDY MET DINO at Stone's house.

Dino was surprised to see him. "You're Felix Dressler again?"

"It's a long story. Everything set on your end?"

"Pretty much. The handler's getting antsy. Wants to know when he can go home."

"Probably tomorrow, but you can't tell him that."

"It seems like there's a lot of things I can't tell people."

"That's what the spy business is all about. Is the prefect going along?"

"He sees the wisdom of catching the Syrians at the handler's house, but he still likes the idea of stopping them at the airport."

"You pointed out that a photo op on the runway would tip off the Syrians, whereas a nice shot of the Paris prefect marching René Darjon off in handcuffs would be all over the evening news."

"I think I phrased it a little more tactfully."

"I'm sure you did," Teddy said. "And you suggested obtaining a search warrant for René Darjon's safe?"

"Yes, I did. He wanted to know why."

"And you said it was so *you* wouldn't have to take credit for it."

"That seemed to be the best answer."

"Okay, I got the time for him. It's eleven o'clock. He should hit the handler's house, the doctor's lab, and René Darjon's office exactly at eleven."

"I'll pass it along."

"Okay, I won't see you again until it's over. If you want to grab a ride home on the Strategic Services jet, I'm sure they wouldn't mind."

"Are you flying with them?"

"Not likely," Teddy said. "I wouldn't want to get in a discussion with the handler."

"I see your point. I think I'll fly commercial, too. If we're on the same flight, should I acknowledge you?"

Teddy smiled. "If you recognize me."

89.

FAHD AND AZIZ waited on the runway in front of hanger forty-seven.

A panel van drove up and the handler and the goons got out.

"Where's the dog?" Fahd said.

The handler jerked his thumb. "In the van." He led Fahd around to the back and pointed through the window. The dog was in a crate.

"Take him out," Fahd said.

"Not on the runway," the hangar pilot said. "You drive the van into the hangar and load the dog. Then I'll tow the plane out for you to board."

"You don't leave until we do," Fahd told the handler.

"We'll wait until the plane is away, in case there is any problem," the handler said.

"Good," Fahd said. "Load the dog."

The handler and the goons got back in the van and drove into the hangar. The handler slipped a leash on the dog's collar and let him out of the van. The goons folded up the crate, carried it onto the plane, and set it up. The handler put the dog in the crate, and threw in a couple of treats. While the dog gobbled them up, he draped a blanket over the crate.

"Night, night, Rocky."

The handler and the goons left the dog on the plane and drove out of the hangar.

THE LUGGAGE HATCH opened and Teddy Fay crawled out, pushing his backpack ahead of him. He was somewhat cramped from having been in the compartment for more than an hour. He stood up, stretched, and lifted up the blanket.

"Hi, Barkley. How you doing?"

Teddy had treats in his hand. Barkley slurped them gratefully. Teddy took a leash out of his backpack, opened the crate door, and snapped the leash on Barkley's collar. He let the dog out of the crate, told him to sit, and gave him a treat.

Teddy shoved his backpack into the crate, closed the door, and draped the blanket back down over it.

Teddy pushed the hatch open wide, and with a handful of treats, led the dog into the baggage compartment. He closed the hatch behind him, plunging them into darkness.

"Easy, boy. It's okay."

A sudden jarring told him the pilot had hooked up the tow to pull the jet out of the hangar. He could feel the plane start to move.

Teddy pushed the hatch open and dropped to the ground.

"Come on, boy. Jump!"

Barkley leapt off the plane. Teddy caught him and helped him land gently and quietly.

The jet was moving away. Teddy slammed the luggage hatch. He pulled Barkley off to one side, out of the line of sight.

FAHD WAS PRACTICALLY tapping his foot waiting for the jet to be towed into position. Though Kristin had assured him everything was fine, Fahd didn't believe in tempting fate. Hanging out on a runway was not a good idea. "No nonsense taking off," he told the pilot. "You don't need to go through a lot of procedures, just start the plane and go. Once we're in the air you can do anything you like. Just get it off the ground."

"As soon as it's ready," the pilot said.

The hangar pilot unhitched the tow and opened the cabin door. "All set. Go ahead and board."

"Come on, come on," Fahd said, herding Aziz ahead of him. "Let's go."

The Syrians boarded the plane and took their seats. The pilot climbed into the cockpit.

"Well, come on, start the engine," Fahd said.

"They're loading your luggage. I can't start the engine until they're clear."

"What's keeping them?"

"They're loading it now."

The hangar pilot closed the cargo door.

"Okay, they're finished," the pilot said. "Sit down and buckle up. Here we go."

Fahd returned to his seat. Before he sat down he looked at the crate in the back of the plane. It was covered by a blanket.

"Check the dog," he said to Aziz.

Without changing expression, the little man managed to look put upon. He got up, and went to the back of the plane. He lifted the blanket off the crate.

He blinked. The dog was gone!

Fahd turned in his seat to look at the dog. Aziz looked stricken. He pulled a backpack out of the crate.

"What's that?" Fahd demanded. "Where's the dog?"

Aziz reached into the backpack and pulled out a package. His eyes widened in alarm. He held it up for Fahd to see.

It was plastic explosives with a remote-control detonator.

CROUCHED IN THE bay doors of the hangar, holding on tightly to the dog, Teddy Fay pushed the button on his cell phone.

The plane blew up.

90.

A SQUAD OF police officers burst into René Darjon's office. Paris Prefect Clement Moreau came striding in after them, a triumphant smile on his face. "René Darjon, I have a warrant for your arrest."

René Darjon's mouth fell open. He rose from his chair in astonishment. "On what charge?"

"Terrorism. Treason. Murder. There are more, but those are probably the ones you will be most concerned with. After you've been convicted of treason, it's hard to focus on your other charges."

"Have you lost your mind?"

"Not at all. At this very moment, my men are arresting Dr. von Heinrich in his laboratory, as well as seizing the dog and arresting the Syrian buyers. By the time they get done talking, you'll be a very sorry individual."

The prefect's cocky boast was only half-true. His men were indeed seizing the doctor, but his other squad had just burst in on an empty house. He was lucky he had another string for his bow.

"It's their word against mine. You've got nothing against me."

The prefect pointed his finger at the framed picture of René Darjon and the prime minister. "Get that wall safe open."

91.

TEDDY AND BARKLEY walked out the main gate. With a plane burning on the runway, no one noticed them.

Dino was waiting in his car. He helped Teddy load Barkley into the crate he'd just purchased, and they took off.

"The prefect's going to be pissed," Dino said.

"Not as pissed as he would have been if he'd stopped the plane. He'd have caught the Syrians with no dog."

"I know it, and you know it, but he doesn't know it, and that's why he's going to be pissed."

"Well," Teddy said, "it's a good thing we're leaving Paris."

"You didn't tell me we'd be leaving ahead of the posse."

"It's not as bad as all that, Dino. He's still got a case against René Darjon, which I'm sure matters more to him than all the Syrians in the world put together. They may not have the dog, but they're squeezing his scientist, who's bound to roll over on him. And there's sure to be a paper trail linking René Darjon to the virus."

"'There's sure to be'?" Dino said.

"Count on it."

Dino pulled up in front of the apartment. Teddy got the dog out of the crate, walked him upstairs, and knocked on the apartment door.

The handler opened it.

"Hi," Teddy said. "I just took Barkley out for a walk. Here he is. He seems fine."

The handler stared at him. "What the hell!"

"And I've got good news. You can go home."

The handler was looking back and forth from Barkley to Rocky. "But . . . But . . ."

"Oh, and you're taking two dogs home. If there's an extra charge, it's all right, just put it on the bill. We got another crate. It's out in the car. I hope the dogs get along. I'm sure they will. They're both pretty easygoing."

The handler was dumbfounded.

"So, I'll take you to the airport this afternoon. You could go now, but it's a little busy out there. And it's the absolute wrong time to show up with a dog."

Teddy smiled. "Enjoy your stay in Paris?"

92.

MILLIE MET LANCE on the White House lawn.

"Our friend is coming home."

"Oh?"

"He found the mole."

"Really?"

"Her name is Kristin Rowan. The Syrian agents brought her onto their payroll to ensure the CIA wouldn't interfere with an international conspiracy taking place at l'Arrington."

"At l'Arrington? Does Stone know that?"

"He will. It's in no way his or Marcel DuBois's fault. A convention for the preservation of endangered species turned out to be a front for a biological weapons deal. That's why finding the mole was just the tip of the iceberg. The real mission was putting the terrorists out of operation."

"And I couldn't have been told this?"

"*I* didn't know. He only tells me what he wants me to know. Or rather what he wants *you* to know. So, the good news is the Syrians have been neutralized and the threat of a biological weapon has been erased. Even if no one knows it. At least, no one but you."

"Yet conveniently there's no proof any of this occurred."

"Well, there will be."

"What!?"

"Our friend is sending the sample of the virus back to you for our scientists to study and create a vaccine. Along with the dog. Your friend's dog is fine. The other dog needs an operation."

"'Other dog'?"

"Luckily the dog's not infected. The virus is in a vial sewn into the lining of the dog's stomach. A simple operation can remove the vial, and the dog will be good to go. Which is nice because Barkley seems to like him. Your friend may wind up with two dogs."

Lance blinked. "Run that by me again."

93.

TEDDY FINISHED SWIMMING laps. He climbed out of his pool, dried off, and relaxed in a deck chair.

His cell phone rang. He picked it up. "Hello?"

It was Lance. "Do you know who this is?"

"How did you find me? I have a new phone with a new number."

"I'm head of the CIA."

"I suppose you have some resources."

Lance exhaled. "Do you do things just to annoy me?"

"Did I send you to Paris on a hopeless mission?"

"It wasn't hopeless. You actually did it."

"And yet you sound annoyed."

"Well, why you couldn't have done it without buying a half-million-euro rhinoceros is beyond me."

"I don't know what you're grousing about. I saved you 275 million dollars on the dog."

"Did I ask you to buy an infected dog?"

"He's not infected."

"So why am I reading reports of how the Paris police foiled an international arms deal involving bioterrorists?"

"You wanted the glory? I thought you guys didn't deal in that. Well, you can blame Dino. He let the prefect take credit in exchange for doing all he wanted. It seemed a fair exchange to me, but you be the judge.

"What you can take credit for is the rhinoceros. The Tanzanian government is eternally grateful to the CIA for their generous donation of a rare black rhino. That gesture bought an awful lot of goodwill."

"A half million euros' worth?"

"Have you seen that rhino? He's a real heartbreaker."

Teddy could practically hear Lance gnashing his teeth.

"You have one more expense."

"Oh, Christ, what else did you buy?"

"Agent Workman was collateral damage. You can't acknowledge how he actually died, so you can make anything up. He was killed in the line of duty, and should be singled out for bravery. If he has a family, they should be generously compensated."

"How did he actually die?"

"I shot him."

Lance sucked in his breath. "Why are you telling me this?"

"So you'll never ask me again. Hang on a minute. I've got another call."

"You're putting the director of the CIA on hold?"

"Because I'm a nice guy. A jerk would hang up on you."

Teddy silenced Lance's angry protests by pressing the hold button, and picked up the other call. "Hello?"

It was Peter Barrington. "Billy. I heard you were back. Want to make a movie?"

"Hell yes," Teddy said. "Let me put you on hold a second, Peter. I've got to get rid of a pest."

Author's Note

I am happy to hear from readers, but you should know that if you write to me in care of my publisher, three to six months will pass before I receive your letter, and when it finally arrives it will be one among many, and I will not be able to reply.

However, if you have access to the Internet, you may visit my website at www.stuartwoods.com, where there is a button for sending me e-mail. So far, I have been able to reply to all my e-mail, and I will continue to try to do so.

If you send me an e-mail and do not receive a reply, it is probably because you are among an alarming number of people who have entered their e-mail address incorrectly in their mail software. I have many of my replies returned as undeliverable.

Remember: e-mail, reply; snail mail, no reply.

When you e-mail, please do not send attachments, as I *never* open these. They can take twenty minutes to download, and they often contain viruses.

Please do not place me on your mailing lists for funny stories, prayers, political causes, charitable fund-raising, petitions, or sentimental claptrap. I get enough of that from people I already know. Generally speaking, when I get e-mail addressed to a large number of people, I immediately delete it without reading it.

Please do not send me your ideas for a book, as I have a policy of writing only what I myself invent. If you send me story ideas, I will immediately delete them without reading them. If you have a good idea for a book, write it yourself, but I will not be able to advise you on how to get it published. Buy a copy of *Writer's Market* at any bookstore; that will tell you how.

Anyone with a request concerning events or appearances may e-mail it to me or send it to: Publicity Department, Penguin Random House LLC, 1745 Broadway, New York, NY 10019.

Those ambitious folk who wish to buy film, dramatic, or television rights to my books should contact Matthew Snyder, Creative Artists Agency, 9830 Wilshire Boulevard, Beverly Hills, CA 98212–1825.

Those who wish to make offers for rights of a literary nature should contact Anne Sibbald, Janklow & Nesbit, 445 Park Avenue, New York, NY 10022. (Note: This is not an invitation for you to send her your manuscript or to solicit her to be your agent.)

If you want to know if I will be signing books in your city, please visit my website, www.stuartwoods.com, where the tour schedule will be published a month or so in advance. If you wish me to do a book signing in your locality, ask your favorite bookseller to contact his Penguin representative or the Penguin publicity department with the request.

If you find typographical or editorial errors in my book and feel an irresistible urge to tell someone, please write to Sara Minnich at Penguin's address above. Do not e-mail your discoveries to me, as I will already have learned about them from others.

A list of my published works appears in the front of this book and on my website. All the novels are still in print in paperback and can be found at or ordered from any bookstore. If you wish to obtain hardcover copies of earlier novels or of the two nonfiction books, a good used-book store or one of the online bookstores can help you find them. Otherwise, you will have to go to a great many garage sales.

Teddy Fay is back in Hollywood and caught in two tricky situations. The first when Centurion star Tessa Tweed becomes the target of malicious gossip, and Teddy must neutralize the source before the situation gets out of hand. The second when Teddy finds himself up against a local mob boss, a guy who took over the family business when his uncle died under mysterious circumstances . . . circumstances that Teddy may have engineered.

1.

TEDDY FAY WOKE up to the sound of breaking glass. He grabbed the remote control from the nightstand and clicked on the monitor of the high-tech security system Mike Freeman had installed in his house. A dozen views appeared showing the exterior, a red dot pinpointing the source of the break-in. Another click of a button and the image moved to fill the screen, and Teddy could see a burly man attempting to get through the living room window. He was being thwarted by a second pane of glass far sturdier than the one he'd just broken.

Teddy grabbed a gun, slipped down the stairs, out a side door, crept up on the man, and jabbed the gun in his back.

The man whirled around and lunged for the gun.

Teddy groaned. Really? If Teddy had wanted to shoot him, the man would be dead. A mere robber wouldn't take that chance. Was he a hired assassin, or just dumb?

Teddy spun around and chopped down on his arm. The intruder howled in pain, but he wasn't done. He shoved his wounded hand into his pocket and came out with a snub-nosed revolver.

Teddy almost felt sorry for him. The man's hand was numb, and he could hardly hold the gun. Teddy batted it away.

Three armored security vans roared up the driveway. A squad of Strategic Services agents poured out, guns drawn.

"Relax, gentlemen," Teddy said. "The situation seems to be in hand."

A young agent who appeared to be in charge said, "You're Billy Barnett?"

"At your service."

"Your system registered a security breach. Is this the intruder?"

"That he is."

"We'd be happy to take him off your hands."

"I doubt if you'll have him long. The system is also linked to the police. I believe that's them now."

A police car came up the drive with its red-and-blue lights flashing. A uniformed officer climbed out of the driver's seat, surveilled the scene, and said laconically, "What's all this?"

"Attempted B&E," Teddy said. "I'm the homeowner. That's the intruder. These gentlemen are private security guards who responded to my alarm."

The officer turned to the agent. "You apprehended the intruder in the attempt to break and enter?"

The agent shook his head. "The homeowner apprehended the intruder."

"Before you got here?"

"That's right."

The cop turned back to Teddy. "So you're the only witness to the attempted break-in?"

"Aside from the alarm system he activated."

"There's no evidence *he* activated the alarm system."

"Actually there is. This is a Strategic Services system, with all the bells and whistles, including cameras. Here, take a look." Teddy led the officer over to the front door. "The main control is in the master bedroom, but this is the downstairs terminal." He pointed to a screen on the wall, and activated the control panel beneath it. An image immediately appeared on the screen, along with the graphic, Front Left Window. The intruder had just smashed the outer window and gone to work on the inner. As the cop watched, he could see Teddy creeping up on the intruder and handily disarming him.

"There you are, officer," Teddy said. "As you can see, it was an armed B&E. I'll give you a thumb drive of the video for evidence."

"You have a gun?"

"I have a permit for it."

"Good. Bring it down to the station with you, and you can swear out a complaint."

Teddy glanced at his watch. "I'll drop by later. Right now I've got a party to go to."

"A party? It's four in the morning."

"Yeah, the party's at five." Teddy smiled. "Good thing the guy woke me up. I might have been late."

2.

I T WAS STILL dark when Teddy pulled his 1958 D Model Porsche Speedster to a stop in front of Peter and Hattie Barrington's house. He skipped up the front steps and rang the bell.

Peter Barrington opened the door. "Come in, the gang's all here. The TV's on and they're about to start."

"Relax. It's the technical awards first. They don't get to the real thing until five thirty."

"I'll be sure to tell lighting and set design what you think of them," Peter said dryly.

Teddy followed Peter out onto the veranda, where Hattie was sitting with Ben and Tessa.

Peter's wife Hattie was a gifted composer and pianist, and had scored Peter's latest movie, among others.

Ben Bacchetti was the head of the studio. He was also Peter's best friend of many years. Their fathers, Stone Barrington and Dino Bacchetti, were also best friends.

Tessa Tweed Bacchetti had come to the studio as an aspiring young actress. She was now a star, and Ben Bacchetti's wife.

Teddy had been in England for Peter and Hattie and

Ben and Tessa's double wedding. The young newlyweds were only partly aware of the role he had played in seeing it went off without a hitch.

"There he is," Tessa said. "I told you he'd be here."

"Sorry I'm late," Teddy said. "Someone tried to rob me."

"Rob you?" Ben said.

Teddy shrugged. "Rob me or kill me, I'm not sure which. The police are asking him now."

Tessa grinned. "Would you stop being so maddeningly casual? You may take these things in stride, but robbing and killing is not really that routine."

"Well, I certainly hope to learn more about it, but the police have taken it out of my hands. The robber couldn't get through Mike Freeman's security system, but he sure set off enough alarms. The poor guy never knew what hit him."

"I'll bet," Ben said.

"But don't let me spoil Oscar nominations morning. I was just explaining why I was late."

"The only thing that could spoil Oscar morning," Hattie said, "is having a nervous breakdown waiting for it."

"Who's nervous?" Peter said. "No one's nervous."

"No one, I'm sure." Hattie smiled teasingly. "Has anyone else noticed who hasn't sat down once since everyone arrived?"

"I'm the host," Peter said. "I'm greeting my guests."

"I can attest to that," Teddy said. "I arrived. He greeted me. He was a little concerned by my tardiness, but I wouldn't characterize it as being nervous."

Peter put up his hands. "Yes, yes, we can all play it cool. But it is the Oscars. Before they get going, let me say this."

Peter took a breath. "I think it's great we could get together this morning to celebrate our film. But while awards are nice, that's not why we do this. We're not out to win awards, only to make good movies. If we can do that, and turn out a film we can be proud of, we don't need outside validation. We know we've done a good job. You all know how I feel about you, and awards or not, I'm very pleased with how this all turned out."

"Well, that's gracious and self-deprecating," Ben said with a grin. "In case you don't remember, your picture just won a Golden Globe. An Oscar nomination is not such a long shot."

"It won for Best *Drama*," Peter said. "At the Globes you're only competing with half the films. There's a strong field of comedies this year."

Hattie laughed. "Would someone nominate him already, before this naysayer ruins the whole party?"

Hattie got the first nomination for Best Original Score. The announcement was cause for jubilation. Hattie had been passed over by the Golden Globes. Peter had reassured her that the Golden Globe voters weren't necessarily the most knowledgeable in the category, and Oscar voters would know better. He was delighted to have been proven right.

"What did I tell you?" Peter said.

"Oh God," Hattie said. "Now we're going to have to listen to him take credit for my nomination all morning."

Peter had his own nominations to brag about. He scored two, for Best Original Screenplay and Best Director.

Finally they got to the acting categories. Best Supporting Actor was first. Stuntman character actor Mark Weldon got a nod for his turn as villain Leonard Kirk.

"Too bad he's not here," Teddy said, and everyone laughed.

There was a tense moment when they got to best actress. None of the first four names were Tessa Tweed. For the first time all morning, the room was deathly quiet.

"And Tessa Tweed," the announcer said, "For *Desperation at Dawn*."

The announcement was met with relief, laughter, and applause.

"Told you so," Teddy said

"You realize this ups her price for your next film," Ben kidded Peter.

Peter smiled. "What are you telling *me* for? You're head of the studio."

"Oh, hell."

After all that, it was almost an anticlimax when the film was nominated for Best Picture.

3.

ON THE OTHER side of town, Viveca Rothschild, dubbed the Blonde Bombshell by the press, was hosting a similar Oscar party. Twenty-nine, lithe, blonde, and voluptuous, Viveca had already racked up two nominations in her career, but had never won. After a lifetime of playing femme fatales, her departure role in a romantic comedy had been a gamble, but it had paid off. Dancing, singing, and delivering big laughs, she had wowed the critics with her versatility, earning her best reviews ever. After taking home her first Golden Globe for Best Actress in a Musical or Comedy, an Oscar nomination was all but assured.

Viveca couldn't have been more nervous. Only the presence of her Hollywood friends and her fiancé Bruce were helping her hold it together. Or at least put up the appearance.

On the television, the presenter said, "The nominations for Best Screenplay are . . ."

The announcement was met by boos, hisses, and cat calls.

Viveca's best friend Cheryl threw a napkin at the screen. "How many damn categories are there?" she said, and everyone laughed.

"Don't worry, honey," Bruce said. "I know you're going to be nominated."

Viveca put up her hand tolerantly, urging her boyfriend to be quiet. Bruce was a handsome young man with rippled muscles and a charming smile, and had been her high school sweetheart. But he was not good at picking up social cues. Bruce had been wounded in Iraq and come home with a Purple Heart, a Medal of Honor, and the resultant post-traumatic stress disorder. For the most part he had a pleasant nature, but as far as his girlfriend was concerned he was ready to fly to her defense at the slightest provocation.

The screenwriter's nominations gave way to Best Directors.

"Did anybody act in these movies?" Cheryl said, and everybody laughed.

As if he heard her, the presenter said, "And the nominees for Best Supporting Actress are . . ."

"*Supporting*!" Cheryl wailed. "Kill me now!"

Finally they got to Best Actress. Three names were read, none of them Viveca's. Fourth time was the charm.

"Viveca Rothschild, for *Paris Fling*."

The entourage burst into roars of approval.

"Quiet, quiet!" Viveca said. "One more to go!"

The room was instantly hushed, with everyone thinking the same thing.

Viveca murmured it under her breath. "*Not* Meryl Streep! *Not* Meryl Streep!"

"And Tessa Tweed, for *Desperation at Dawn*," the presenter said, and the room collectively sighed in relief.

Viveca had dodged that one last bullet.

The Oscar was within her grasp.

4.

CHAZ BOWEN EYED the attorney suspiciously. He had no reason to. The attorney, Richard Fitzgerald, was a slick shyster who represented a number of mobsters and crime bosses in the Los Angeles area. Which was exactly the type of lawyer Chaz needed, only Chaz was too dumb to know it.

Chaz was a sullen man, with hostile eyes, who suspected no one liked him. He was not entirely wrong on that count.

"Who the hell are you?"

"I'm your attorney, Mr. Bowen. I'm here to get you out."

"Well, you took your time getting here," Chaz snarled.

"You made the mistake of getting arrested in the middle of the night. The system works slower then."

"Can I go home?"

"What'd you tell the cops?"

"Told 'em I wanted a lawyer."

"Anything else?"

"Hell, no."

"You didn't try to give them a reason why you were trying to break into a Hollywood producer's house?"

"Couldn't think of one. Can you?"

"So what happened?"

"How the hell should I know? A simple break-in and a fucking SWAT team shows up. What the hell is that all about?"

FITZGERALD WENT OUT and hunted up the Assistant District Attorney assigned to the case.

"Hey, Jason. Wanna play let's make a deal?"

"Ricky Fitz. How the hell are you?"

"Pissed, that's how. I was up at the crack of dawn to come down here just to bail a guy out."

"What's the case?"

"Chaz Bowen."

"Oh, that one. Slam dunk. Caught in the act with burglar tools and a gun. Breaking into a Hollywood producer's house, for Christ's sake."

"Was he arrested in the house?"

"He was apprehended while trying to get in the window."

"So you can't charge him with breaking and entering. He didn't enter."

"I can charge him with attempted burglary."

"You'll never get a conviction."

"Give me a break. You're going to cop a plea and you know it. You can't put that guy in front of a jury. If he answers questions, he's guilty. If he refuses to answer questions, he's guilty. The minute he steps into court, he's guilty."

"My client doesn't want to serve time."

"Then he shouldn't have gotten arrested."

"I couldn't agree more. Shall we pretend he didn't?"

"Unfortunately he's been booked."

"You can always drop the charges."

"With so much evidence? My boss would want to know why. His-lawyer-told-me-to is a very poor answer."

"I gotta get him out."

The A.D.A. shook his head. "You cop a plea, he's doing time. I can't give you a deal where he doesn't."

"How about time served?"

"A half an hour? Come on, Ricky, the charge isn't going away. The only way he's gets out is on bail."

"How much?"

DONNIE MARTEL SNATCHED up the phone. "Yeah?"

"Donnie. Rick Fitzgerald. You sent me to bail out Chaz."

"Did you do it?"

"Sure thing."

"How much?"

"Hundred thousand."

"That much?"

"The guy had a gun on him, Donnie. He's lucky he's out at all."

"Did he talk?"

"If he had, he'd have talked himself into a cell. The

guy's a moron, Donnie. Shutting up is the only bright thing he's ever done."

"Are you kidding me? The guy's an expert locksmith."

"That is the type of thing I don't want to know, Donnie."

"Why didn't he talk?"

"He couldn't think of anything to say."

"Jesus."

DONNIE SLAMMED DOWN the phone. Donnie Martel was a lower level crime boss with big aspirations and little to show for it. He was always eager to do jobs for the big boys, the shit jobs that no one wanted to do but everyone needed done. He did a lot of them, and most of them panned out. When they came off without a hitch, they were completely unappreciated. No one ever noticed his efforts until something fucked up. In Donnie's case it was always baby steps forward, and a gigantic slide back.

Chaz Morton was one hell of a slide. The situation couldn't have been worse. Here he was, doing a job for the one guy on the west coast he wanted to impress. Gino Patelli was the big boss, the legit boss, the one the others all kowtowed to, the one who was never personally involved in anything.

Donnie couldn't believe it had all gone wrong. It had been such a simple job. Yes, it was a hit, but it was an easy hit, not like whacking some rival mob boss. It was a movie producer, for God's sake, Mr. John Q. Public. This wasn't a complicated scenario, just a home invasion gone bad. The stupidest thug in the world could pull that off.

But, no, Donnie had to find one even stupider. So now he had to tell Gino Patelli the simple assignment the big man had condescended to give him had blown up in his face.

Donnie picked up the phone to make the call. He started punching in the number, when he found his hand shaking. He slammed down the receiver.

Damn.

This would have to be done in person.

STUART WOODS

"Addictive . . . Pick it up at your peril.
You can get hooked."
—*Lincoln Journal Star*

For a complete list of titles and to sign up for our
newsletter, please visit prh.com/StuartWoods